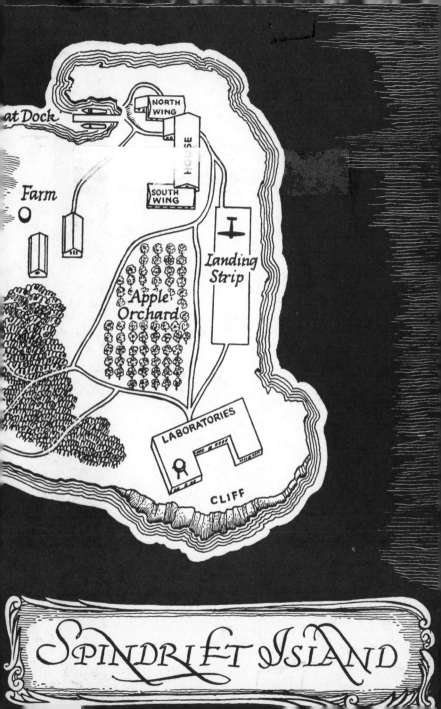

THE ROCKET'S SHADOW

The RICK BRANT SCIENCE-ADVENTURE *Stories*

BY JOHN BLAINE

———•••———

There, on the roof of the barn, was the message!

THE ROCKET S SHADOW

A RICK BRANT ELECTRONIC ADVENTURE

THE ROCKET'S SHADOW

By JOHN BLAINE

GROSSET & DUNLAP PUBLISHERS

NEW YORK, N. Y.

Contents

THE ROCKET'S SHADOW

CHAPTER I

The Unforeseen

RICK BRANT, being tall for his age, had no trouble making the final connections on his latest invention. He screwed the bell on solidly, then stepped back to view his handiwork.

The doorbell was now in an unusual position. Instead of being at waist level, it had been moved to the inside of the doorframe and placed up high.

It looked fine. A stranger might have to hunt a little before he saw the push button, but he'd find it all right. Rick went inside and threw the switch that would send electricity into the gadget and then went to collect the family.

Mrs. Brant was in the kitchen, supervising the supper preparations for the family and for the scientists who made their home on Spindrift Island.

Rick sampled the cake frosting in a near-by bowl and invited:

1

"Come out to the porch for a minute, Mom? There's something I want to show you."

Mrs. Brant looked up from the roast she was seasoning, a twinkle in her eyes. "What is it now, Rick? Another invention?"

"Wait and see," he said mysteriously. "I'll go get Dad and Barby."

He hurried into the big front room that Hartson Brant used as an office. It was filled with books written in several languages, all of them on scientific subjects. One wall was covered with framed degrees stating that Hartson William Brant was an engineer, a Master of Arts, a member of numerous scientific societies, and a Fellow of the American Institute of Atomic Scientists.

In the center of the room was a massive desk, littered now with blueprints, wiring diagrams, and stacks of paper that were covered with obscure mathematical figures.

Hartson Brant, clad in an unprofessorlike slack suit, and with his brown hair mussed, was scowling over an intricate equation.

Rick waited until his father looked up, not wanting to break into his train of thought.

In many ways, Rick Brant was a younger edition of his famous father. Both were slender, with brown hair and eyes, and Rick had inherited his father's dislike of "dressing up." He was usually dressed in a pair of worn slacks and a sweater, with moccasins for footgear.

"What is it, son?" Hartson Brant asked finally.

"I have something to show you if you're not too busy, Dad."

Hartson Brant rose, pushing back his chair with relief. "Just for a minute," he agreed. "It will give me a chance to rest before I go back to this confounded equation."

"Is it tough?" Rick asked sympathetically.

"Worse than that. It's the blast-reaction equation for the rocket. I'm rechecking Zircon's figures. Well, what is it this time? A new electric shoe polisher?"

Rick's shoe polisher was a standing joke in the family. It had worked, all right, but too well. The clamp that held the shoe in place while the automatic brush went over it had stuck firmly, but by the time the power could be cut off, most of the leather had been worn from the shoe he had borrowed for a demonstration.

"This one works," he promised. "It's on the front porch. I'll get Barby; then we'll try it."

He went to the foot of the stairs and yelled, "Hey, brat! Come on down."

His mother appeared from the kitchen. "Isn't Barby at the telephone switchboard?"

"She never is," Rick said. "A fine telephone operator she is."

He grinned as a slender, blond girl, a year younger

than he, came down the stairs. She walked with a conscious effort at gracefulness, her head held high and her face set in a frozen expression that seemed to indicate worldly boredom.

"Did someone call me?" she asked languidly.

"Today she is being Ethel Barrymore," Rick told his smiling parents. "I recognize the pose. Come on, brat. I have something to show you."

The pose was dropped instantly and Barbara Brant came down the remaining stairs in a rush. "Is it a new invention, Rick?"

"The Brant Identification Panel," he replied. "Wait till you see it."

"Lead us to it, Rick," Hartson Brant said dryly.

Rick led the way to the front porch, closing the door behind him.

Mrs. Brant looked closely at the door. "Rick, what on earth—"

"Watch," he said. "Barby, ring the doorbell."

The girl's hand reached out toward the spot where the button had been, but stopped short. "It's gone!" she exclaimed.

Rick pointed to the new location, high on the doorframe. "There it is."

Mr. and Mrs. Brant exchanged glances.

Barby looked doubtful, but by standing on tiptoe she could just reach it. As her finger touched the button there was a sharp crash and a panel about six inches square swung out of the door. She jumped back with a little squeal of fright.

The shaggy little dog that had joined them, and was watching curiously, let out a surprised yelp. Barby bent down swiftly. "Did I step on you, Diz?"

Dismal, pleased with the attention, promptly rolled over and played dead, all four legs in the air.

"See?" Rick said, grinning. "Even Diz is impressed."

"It's wonderful," Mrs. Brant said doubtfully. "What is it?"

"Suppose you're upstairs. Someone comes to the door and rings the bell. The panel drops out." Rick opened the door and pointed to a mirror. "The reflection is picked up. There's another mirror on the landing, and still another one at the head of the stairs. It's like a periscope. You can see who's at the door without coming down."

His mother was puzzled, his father amused, and Barby looked pleased.

"What a wonderful idea!" she exclaimed. She ran up the stairs and in a moment called down excitedly, "I can see all of you. It's perfect, Rick!"

Mrs. Brant shook her head. "But wouldn't it be much easier just to look out the window?"

Hartson Brant spoke up. "We mustn't discourage him, dear. This thing has definite possibilities, especially

the new bell location. Just think, if a midget brush sales-
man comes, he won't be able to reach it."

Rick looked sharply at his father. It was hard to tell
when the scientist, usually serious, was joking. Then he
saw the suspicious twinkle in Mr. Brant's eyes.

"Aw, Dad, that isn't the idea at all."

"I'm not poking fun at your invention," Hartson Brant
assured him. "It's very fine. Or it would be, if we ever
had strangers calling at the house."

"I didn't think of that," Rick answered, abashed. It
was true that strangers never rang the doorbell. That
was because the location of the big Brant house on
Spindrift Island made it almost impossible for casual
visitors to drop in. They had to be brought by boat from
the town of Whiteside, on the mainland.

Barby came back downstairs and hurried to her
brother's defense. "I think it's wonderful. Why, Rick is
just like—like Edison, or something."

"I've never doubted it," Hartson Brant assured her
with a smile. "Incidentally, this clears up a mystery.
I've wondered what happened to that spare photo-
electric cell we had at the lab."

"I meant to tell you I borrowed it," Rick confessed.
"Want to see how the panel works?"

He explained it with a certain pride. The photo-
electric cell was set just below the doorbell. When the
button was pushed it turned on a small light that op-

erated the cell, which in turn released the catch that held the door panel in place.

"It's very ingenious," Mrs. Brant said. "Thank you for showing me, Rick. Now, you'll have to excuse me or I won't have supper ready on time."

As Mrs. Brant went into the house, she looked at the hole in the door panel, but she didn't say anything.

"What's for supper, Mom?" Barby called after her.

From inside came a sudden loud buzzing. "The switchboard," Barby exclaimed, and hurried off. She had volunteered to handle the island's switchboard, but after a week of sitting at the board, she had persuaded Rick to install a buzzer that could be heard all over the house. Now it was a usual sight to see her running for the board from some remote part of the house.

Rick and his father were left alone. Even Dismal had gone, sniffing his excitement at the scent of the roast.

"I guess it isn't very practical, Dad, but I had fun figuring it out," Rick said.

"That's the idea, son. A scientist has to be practical, but only up to a point. You'll probably work out dozens of ideas before you find a useful one. And even the biggest thing you ever do might not seem practical to some people."

"Like the rocket, Dad?"

"That's right. Sending a rocket to the moon probably seems like an impractical stunt to most people."

Rick walked with his father back to the office. "Maybe they'll change their minds when they see what happens. It won't be long now."

"A week should do it, always barring the unforeseen. We're right on schedule in spite of the trouble we've had."

As they crossed into the big office, Rick's thoughts were on his family. They were swell. No matter how silly his tinkering seemed, they were always enthusiastic and considerate. Even his mother had said nothing about the hole he had cut in the front door. And his father, in spite of the many things on his mind, had taken the trouble to look and comment.

The telephone jangled sharply and Hartson Brant picked it up.

"Yes?"

Rick saw his father's face tighten as he replaced the receiver and ran for the door.

"What is it, Dad?"

"The unforeseen," his father answered grimly. "The control panel at the lab just blew out."

CHAPTER II

The Men in the Gray Sedan

RICK hurried after his father through the apple orchard, which separated the stone laboratory buildings from the house.

"What did they say, Dad?"

"Weiss didn't give any details; he just said the panel had blown and to hurry over," Mr. Brant replied.

In a moment they were through the orchard and crossing the lawn in front of the long, low stone building. As they entered the main door, a small, stoop-shouldered man hurried to meet them, rubbing his hands nervously. This was Dr. Julius Weiss, whose undistinguished appearance hid one of the keenest scientific minds in the country.

"It was the relay," Weiss announced. "It failed to throw out and the overload burned out everything on the board."

Rick followed into the inner workroom where the scientists had been working on the rocket-control panel. An electrical relay, he knew, served the same purpose as a fuse. But where a fuse would blow out, the relay would just open the circuit. Only the relay hadn't worked.

In the workroom, two men looked up from their inspection of a blackened mass of glass and wiring. The air was heavy with the odor of burnt insulation.

The two men were of about the same height, but there the similarity ended.

Hobart Zircon, famed electronic scientist, was a huge barrel of a man, bearded of face and bushy of hair. His voice rolled out of his massive chest with the emphasis of a bass drum. He was big, but not fat. His strength was legendary.

John Stringfellow fitted his name. He was lean to the point of gauntness, precise of speech and neat of dress. Even the shapeless laboratory coat he wore seemed to have been tailored for him. The gray eyes set in his thin face were keen and perceptive. He was a wizard at mathematics and a skilled radio technician.

"Take a look at this mess, Hartson," Hobart Zircon boomed. He indicated the burnt panel.

Hartson Brant probed into the wreckage with skilled fingers. "What happened?" he asked.

"We were making a routine test," John Stringfellow

explained. "Julius threw the switch and the panel burned out before we could get to it. If the relay had thrown out when the power overload hit, this wouldn't have happened."

Rick spoke up, framing his question out of the suspicions that had leaped into his mind. "What caused the overload?"

He knew that the electric current generated at the powerhouse next to the lab was a constant 440 volts. It must have risen to a terrific voltage to do so much damage.

"I wish we knew," Stringfellow told him. "I went out and checked the generators as soon as it happened. They registered normal."

"Possibly a power surge on the line from the mainland," Weiss said.

"But there wouldn't be a power surge unless there was a storm, would there?" Rick asked.

"That's beside the point," Hartson Brant said. "Why didn't the relay throw out?"

"We'll soon see," Stringfellow assured him. He was already at work, disconnecting the mechanism. Rick watched as the technician placed the relay on the bench and began tearing it down. The scientists had gathered around and were inspecting each part curiously as it was removed.

Hobart Zircon's sausagelike fingers swooped down

suddenly on a silvery piece of metal. He held it up triumphantly. "Here it is," he exclaimed. "Melted! Defective manufacture. That's what it was!"

He passed the bit of metal around and the scientists nodded in agreement.

"But why didn't it burn out before?" Rick put in hesitantly.

"Questions!" Zircon bellowed. "Always questions from this young man. Why should it burn out before? Under a normal electrical load it would operate. Under an overload, the flaw gives way and it melts. What else?"

"I guess you're right," Rick agreed grudgingly. But he couldn't help thinking that this accident followed closely the pattern of similar mishaps that had taken place during the work on the experiment. The blame had always fallen on defective parts. None of the accidents had been serious, but they had all resulted in lost time—and time was important, now that the experiment was almost at an end.

"John, take a look in the stock room, if you please," Hartson Brant said. "See if we have enough replacements to rebuild this panel."

Stringfellow nodded, and hurried to the small room where extra parts were kept. In a moment he was back.

"We have everything," he announced, "except that triode rectifier tube."

"I can send Rick in by plane for that," Hartson Brant said.

"Maybe we can save him a trip," Stringfellow replied thoughtfully. "I just possibly may have a triode rectifier in my office."

"Would you look and see, John?"

The tall scientist hurried off toward his office and Mr. Brant turned back to the group around the panel. "We'll have to work this evening to make up for the lost time," he told them. "Hobart, will you tear down the panel? Julius, I think we'll want extra relays in the circuit from the powerhouse, in case there is another surge in the main line." He turned to Rick. "I hope John can save you that trip in, son," he said. "These time losses are becoming serious." He looked down the hall toward Stringfellow's office as he spoke, but there was no sign of the thin scientist.

Rick bent low to watch Zircon tear down the panel. As the minutes ticked away, his father paced the floor impatiently.

It was a full twenty minutes before Stringfellow returned. He walked into the room, shaking his head.

"I was sure I had a tube in my office, but I was mistaken. I guess Rick will have to make the trip in, after all."

Hartson Brant gave a shrug of disappointment. "Make

it as fast as you can, will you, Rick?" he said, reaching for his wallet. He peeled off a few bills and handed them to his son and then he scribbled the name and the manufacturer's number of the triode tube on a scrap of paper.

"It's a standard type of tube," he remarked. "Any of the supply houses near by should have them in stock. Better pick up three or four. We want a good supply on hand."

"Okay, Dad. I should be back by suppertime."

"Be careful," his father admonished, "but don't waste time. "We'll need that tube tonight."

Rick ran through the orchard to the house and picked up his flight jacket. Then, telling his mother that he was going on an errand, he hurried to the seaward side of the island.

There on the grassy strip that flanked the orchard sat his pride and joy—a trim, yellow Piper Cub airplane.

He checked it over carefully, tested the controls, and took a look at the fuel stick. Then, after pulling the little propeller through to prime the cylinders, he reached into the cabin to advance the throttle and turn on the switch.

He snapped the propeller down and, thanks to the care he lavished on it daily, the little engine roared into life at once. While the engine warmed, he untied the ropes that protected the plane from sudden winds and kicked the chocks from under the wheels. Then he climbed into the cabin and, with a glance at the home-made windsock dangling from one of the orchard trees, he rolled down the grassy strip and was airborne.

Spindrift Island fell below as he climbed, heading toward the New Jersey shore. The island was roughly oval, except for a hook-shaped cove where two fast mo-torboats rested against the pier. On the seaward side, on opposite corners, were the house and laboratory, the orchard between them. On the south side of the island, about halfway between the sea and the Jersey coast, was a field surrounded by heavy woods, except where it fronted on the water.

Rick's eyes grew speculative as he looked down at Pirate's Field—so named because island legend had it that the woman pirate, Anne Bonney, had once pic-nicked there with her gang of cutthroats. In the center of the field was a tall, canvas-covered structure from which the moon rocket would be launched. Already the base was in place. In a few days, if all went well, the rocket would speed moonward.

A short distance up the coast, as he turned toward the town of Whiteside, he noticed that his oil-pressure gauge was falling off. It had been acting up, owing to some defect in the instrument itself. He was sure he had pressure enough, but there was no use taking a chance. He banked tightly toward the airfield on the edge of town. In a few moments he was setting the Cub down on the gravel strip and taxiing to a stop in front of the hangar.

Gus, manager of the Whiteside Airport, gasoline attendant, mechanic, flight instructor, and philosopher, came out to greet him, rubbing greasy hands on the thighs of his dungarees.

An assistant, whom Rick had seen only a few times, was with him. Gus introduced him as "Mac" and then asked:

"What's up, Rick?"

"The oil-pressure gauge again. I'm afraid to trust it."

Gus turned to Mac. "Take a look in that shipment of parts that came in this morning and see if there's a new gauge. I ordered one a week ago."

Mac went into the hangar and came out in a moment with a cardboard box.

"This the one?"

"That's it," Gus said. "It'll only take a little while to install, Rick. Want me to do it now?"

Rick hesitated. "I have to go to Newark on an errand. Can I borrow your car?"

"Sure," Gus agreed. "Take it. Drive it fast. Maybe hit a tree with it so I can collect the insurance. I need a new one."

Mac, the new attendant, laughed.

"Get someone else to have your accidents." Rick grinned. "I'm a safe-and-sane driver."

"I've seen you drive," Gus chuckled. "You take corners like you were banking the Cub. Go along, sonny. We'll have the gauge in by the time you get back."

Rick climbed into the battered jalopy that stood before the hangar. "Thanks, grandpa," he mocked. Gus was only about three years older than Rick.

He stepped on the starter and the motor groaned protestingly into life. The car rolled out onto the highway and he headed for the manufacturing area on the outskirts of Newark. He knew just where to go for the tube—he had been on many similar errands for the scientists.

He left Whiteside behind, thinking that Gus evidently put in more time on the jalopy than he did on his planes. It rattled and complained, but there was surprising power under the battered hood. He stepped on the gas and the old car leaped ahead. But, as he picked up speed, a tire blew with a loud report, followed by a bumping and crunching as the jalopy rolled along on the rim.

Rick pulled up and got out, muttering to himself. Fortunately, there was a spare. There was also a jack that didn't work until he had fussed with it for fifteen minutes. But at last the tire was changed and he rolled on his way again. With the flat, he estimated, the trip to Newark would take more than an hour.

The Farnham Radio and Television Supply Company

was his first stop. The clerk looked at the slip of paper
Rick presented and then said:

"You're half an hour too late, son. We just sold out all
we had—six of 'em. Don't expect any more until some-
time next week."

Rick thanked him and drove to another supply house.
He handed the specifications to the girl at the desk.

"Better give me three of them," he said.

She shook her head. "Sorry. We only had three on
hand, and a man bought those about fifteen minutes
ago."

Rick was disturbed as he drove through traffic to another company. The errand wasn't turning out to be as
simple as he'd thought. When he went into the third
office, he asked, "Do you have any of these?"

"Did have," the man at the supply desk said. "But
we sold them not more than a quarter of an hour ago.
Man came in and asked for all we had."

He went out thoughtfully. There was no reason why
there should be such an unprecedented demand for that
particular tube. With sudden decision, he swung the car
in the direction of the Cotter Electronic Supply Company, on the far side of Newark. Cotter was one of the
biggest supply houses. If anyone had the tubes, certainly they would.

He drew up in front of the brick building and parked
behind a gray sedan of expensive make. As he got out

and walked to the front door, two men in the sedan watched him suspiciously.

Strange-looking men to find in front of an electronic supply house, Rick thought. They looked like prize fighters or wrestlers.

As he went into the front office, a man brushed by. Rick caught a quick glimpse of a short, neat beard and a pair of dark glasses. The man carried a square package under his arm.

Rick greeted the clerk cordially. "How's business, Dick?"

"Okay. What's new on Spindrift Island?"

"Not much," Rick said. "Got any of these?" He handed the clerk the specification slip.

"I'll be doggoned," the clerk exclaimed. "Why all the sudden interest in these things?"

"What sudden interest?" Rick asked quickly.

"I had a dozen in stock," the clerk said. "We'd had them for quite a while—they weren't much in demand. Then, just now a man comes in and buys out the whole stock and you come along and want the same thing."

"What man?" Rick asked sharply.

"Tall guy with a beard. You must have passed him on the way in."

"I did," Rick exclaimed. "Excuse me!" He was out the door before the clerk could say another word.

The gray sedan was just vanishing around the corner.

He jumped into the jalopy and kicked it into action. Something was wrong. Coincidence was all right, but when the sudden demand for a certain tube stretched all over Newark and ended up with a bearded man who bought out entire stocks of tubes . . . Well, that was just too much.

He had seen instantly that the bearded man wasn't in sight. He couldn't have walked to the corner in that time. Rick decided that he must be in the gray sedan. Hurling the jalopy around the corner with tires screaming, he caught a glimpse of the car as it turned into another street farther up.

Rick had no definite plan of action; his following the sedan was only an impulse. But a hunch told him that the bearded man who had bought up all the tubes was in that car.

He was gaining on the gray sedan now. He slowed down, content to keep it in sight.

The gray sedan led him to the outskirts of Newark; then it turned in the direction of Whiteside, speeding up as it hit the open highway. Rick crouched over the wheel and gave the battered airport car all the gas it would take. It pounded like a broken washing machine, but there was enough speed in the ancient motor to keep the sedan in sight.

The car ahead slowed suddenly and Rick had to jam on the brakes to keep from overhauling it. He saw a face pressed to the rear window and knew he had been seen. The men in the sedan would recognize the jalopy as the one that had parked in front of Cotter's.

Suddenly he felt apprehensive. The men hadn't looked like the kind who would take kindly to being trailed.

The car swept into Whiteside, and Rick closed in to keep from losing the sedan in traffic. The gray car spun into a side street, catching him unawares. He turned the jalopy after it, just in time to see the gray sedan sweep into a narrow alley.

Rick jammed on the brakes and went after it at a safer speed, driving the old car cautiously through stacks of crates, garbage cans, and the like. The sedan shot out the far end and turned left. He held to the wheel grimly and followed, realizing that they were trying to shake him. That knowledge only increased his determination. If the men in the sedan were trying to lose him, they must have something to hide.

In the center of Whiteside, the fleeing sedan came to a red light and went right through it without slowing down. Rick gritted his teeth and jabbed down the accelerator. He jerked the wheel over just in time to avoid a truck that was proceeding through the intersection. Behind him, he heard the shrill screech of a police whistle.

His heart went into his boots. Every officer on the

Whiteside force knew the old airport car by sight. Most of them knew Rick, too. But he couldn't stop now. Gus would have to explain it away—if he could.

There was no time to worry about that now. The sedan was streaking for the open country and he had to push the pedal to the floor to keep up. The gray car led the way to a secondary road that headed north along the shore. The highway was deserted as the two cars sped away from Whiteside into wooded country.

Rick worried. Following the gray car had been a senseless thing, when he stopped to think of it. What could he hope to do? There was nothing illegal about the bearded man's buying up all the tubes in sight.

In spite of his realization that he could do nothing, he never slowed his pursuit of the other car. Instead, it was the gray sedan that brought the chase to an unexpected close.

The chase led into a densely wooded section, far from the nearest house. They roared past the solitary figure of a hiker and the road stretched ahead of them, completely deserted.

Then, with a suddenness that caught Rick by surprise, the gray sedan screamed to a stop, turning so that it blocked the road.

CHAPTER III

The Marines Have Landed

Rick slammed the brakes to the floor and the old car bucked to a stop, scarcely ten feet from the gray car. Ahead, the doors of the sedan opened and the three men got out.

One of the men, a squat, flat-nosed man in a derby, came up and said crisply, "Okay, kid. Get out."

Rick obeyed, his heart pounding. As he stepped to the ground, the other two moved close to him. One was the bearded man. The other was thickset, with the long arms and short neck of a wrestler. He wore a sports jacket of bright-colored checks and a battered felt hat. His eyes were close-set, and of a strange, glassy hardness.

The bearded man confronted Rick. "Young man, you have been following us for miles. My friends and I demand to know why."

23

The question put Rick on the defensive. He stammered, "Why, I—that is, I—"

"Out with it, kid," the man in the derby growled. "Why you been shackin' us all over the country?"

Rick put on a bold front, concealing the trembling of his knees. These men looked capable of anything. Even the bearded man, in spite of an almost scholarly appearance, had a thin-lipped mouth that was held in a firm slit.

"You've been buying up all the triode tubes in the area," he said. "I need one badly. Could I buy one?"

The man in the sports coat pushed his face close to Rick's. "We're collectin' 'em and we don't want to sell, see?"

Rick swallowed. "I just thought it was strange. How could you use that many tubes?"

"We use 'em to trim Christmas trees," the man in the derby growled. "Got anything to say about that?"

The three men had been moving gradually closer to him until now he was trapped against the jalopy. He looked from one face to the other and a wave of cold fear came over him. These men were dangerous. He could see it in the wicked gleam of their eyes, in the cruelty of the bearded man's thin lips.

If he could get away, into the woods . . .

There was a space of about five feet between the bearded man and the one in the sports coat. Rick lunged for it, his legs driving hard.

The man in the sports coat grabbed his sleeve, pulled him off balance, and swung him around. Rick brought his foot up in a vicious arc that smashed against the man's thigh muscle. The man let out a cry of agony and rolled on the hard macadam, grabbing at his leg.

But the kick had thrown Rick off balance. As he tee-tered wildly, the man in the derby hit him from behind. Two long arms closed in a circular vise around his chest and lifted him from the ground. The bearded man stepped forward with raised fist, his thin lips drawn back from his teeth.

Both of Rick's arms were pinioned; there was only one thing to do. He threw his head back sharply into his cap-tor's face. There was a muffled grunt and he felt the arms loosen. He tore himself loose and whirled just in time to see a fist streaking toward his face. He ducked—but too late!

His knees buckled as the fist smashed into his fore-head. He staggered back and fought to keep his balance, but the bearded man stuck out a leg and neatly kicked his feet from under him. Before he could get up, the man in the derby had leaped on his chest, crushing the breath from him.

Rick looked dizzily up into the face of his opponent. Suddenly the face was jerked away from him by a lean, brown hand.

Two things happened simultaneously, unbelievably! A strong fist smashed the derby down over the man's eyes, while a side punch with the open hand caught the man under the chin. He crashed to the road.

Rick jerked to his feet. He caught a glimpse of a flashing smile and of a forest-green marine uniform, as he heard the stranger shout, "Watch it!"

The bearded man and the one in the sports coat were advancing toward the two boys with arms extended, their faces set in hard, vicious lines.

Rick took an uncertain step backward. But the marine's hand lanced forward into the bearded man's midriff. The man doubled forward.

The man in the sports coat launched himself in a flying tackle. With a quick, dancing step, the marine dodged. Rick saw his rescuer's arm chop down, aiming the outside edge of his hand like a blade. It landed just where the man's thick neck connected with his shoulders and he dived to the road.

"Let's get out of here," the marine shouted. He grabbed Rick, who stared at him, dumb-struck with the quickness of it. The boys legged it down the road.

Rick knew a thing or two about running, but the ground-eating pace of the marine made him step up his stride to a hard sprint. They ran all-out for a minute, throwing glances over their shoulders.

The three men had picked themselves up and were staring after the two boys.

"In here," the marine motioned. He led the way off

the road into the woods. "I don't think they'll try to follow."

Through the trees they saw the men get into the sedan and drive off, leaving the highway empty except for the airport car. Rick let out a sigh of relief. "They've gone." He turned to his rescuer with a forced grin.

The marine was a husky boy, perhaps an inch taller than Rick. His hair under the green overseas cap was black, his eyes were brown, set in a tanned, friendly face. His green uniform had red sergeant's chevrons on both sleeves and there was a double row of ribbons over the left pocket. A small pack was slung over his shoulders.

"You certainly saved my bacon," Rick said soberly. He held out his hand. "Thanks."

The young marine—he looked scarcely old enough to be in uniform—took Rick's hand in a firm grip. His ready smile flashed. "No strain. It was a good fight—while it lasted." He added, "My name's Don Scott. Scotty, for short."

"Mine's Rick Brant. What did you do? I never saw anything happen so fast."

"Judo punches," Scotty said. "I learned them in the marines." He looked at Rick speculatively. "What was it all about, anyway?"

Rick didn't know how to answer, so he countered with a question of his own. "Where did you drop from?"

"You passed me," Scotty said. "I was hiking along when you sailed by. I saw you stop up the road. Just as I was going by, the fight started, so I took a hand. Three against one didn't look so good."

"If you hadn't . . ." Rick leaned against a sapling, his knees still a bit unsteady. "Where are you heading?"

Scotty shrugged. "Nowhere special. I'm looking for a job. I got discharged in Washington two days ago, so I headed for New York, hitchhiking. I thought maybe I could find something to do in the city."

"Is your home in New York?"

"Don't have a home," Scotty replied cheerfully. "The only relative I had was my grandmother. She passed away while I was overseas."

An idea took form in Rick's head. "Come home with me, Scotty," he suggested. "I'll bet my father can find a job for you."

Scotty hesitated. "Look, I'm not asking any favors just because I took a hand in that scrap."

"That has nothing to do with it," Rick assured him. "We'll go home and you can talk to Dad. You'll like him. He's regular."

"We'd better call the police first, hadn't we?"

"Not now," Rick evaded. "I want to talk to Dad."

They walked back and got into the jalopy. Rick headed it around toward Whiteside.

"Your car?" Scotty asked.

"I borrowed it."

The assorted noises of the car made conversation difficult and the boys fell silent until Rick turned down the road leading to the airport.

"Do you live far from here?" Scotty asked.

"On an island. It's about fifteen minutes away."

"By boat?"

"By air."

The marine stared. "By air? You mean there's an **air** line that flies to where you live?"

They topped the rise in front of the airport and the field spread before them. Rick pointed proudly to his Cub. "That's our air line."

Scotty looked at him with new respect. "You fly it?"

Rick nodded. "The government had a program to teach kids to fly. It wasn't hard."

"Oh, then your dad got you a plane?"

"Not on your life," Rick asserted vigorously. "I worked that deal myself. I formed a company and sold shares, and that gave me enough money to buy the Cub. All the scientists chipped in. Now I pay them back by doing their errands and ferrying them around at reduced rates."

Scotty was puzzled. "What scientists?"

"You'll see," Rick answered.

He stopped the airport car in front of the hangar, warning Scotty with a glance not to mention the fight to Gus.

"Some can!" he said to the mechanic. "When you going to turn it over to the Whiteside museum? And give those tires away. I had a flat."

Gus shook his head sadly. "Listen how he talks about my car. He has no respect for old age, that's what. Mac gassed up the Cub, I think."

"You think? What a way to run an airport. I'd better take a look. Maybe you just *think* you put in the new oil gauge, too!"

"Not on your life," replied Gus. "I did that with my own lily-white hands."

As Rick walked around the plane toward the cabin, he stopped suddenly. The inspection port in the tail assembly, a tiny metal door, was partly open. "Hey, Gus, tell Mac to keep his eyes open, will you? He left the inspection port open." He secured it and climbed in, a little angry. He didn't like people to be careless with his plane.

Scotty got in beside him and they tightened safety belts. Gus pulled the prop through and the engine caught at once. Rick waved his thanks and taxied to the end of the runway. In a moment they were in the air, climbing like a gull toward the sea and home. Rick kept a careful eye on the new oil pressure gauge until he saw that it read normally. He leveled off for the run to Spindrift.

CHAPTER IV

Scotty Gets Himself a Job

RICK flew due east until he picked up the old barn that was his regular landmark, and then banked in a lazy circle over it and set his course for Spindrift Island. He noted absently that a new advertising slogan had been painted on the barn's slanting roof:

SMOKE WHITE CREAM.

"Do you fly a lot?" Scotty asked.

"Every day during the summer," Rick said, "if the weather's good. I'm the island taxi and delivery service. In the winter I fly to school and do the shopping on the way home."

"What do you do the rest of the time?"

"Sometimes I tinker with gadgets. And sometimes Dad lets me help out in the lab. I get a big kick out of that."

"What are these labs?"

31

"I'll show them to you," Rick promised. "But I can't talk about the experiments and stuff without Dad's okay."

He pointed ahead to where Spindrift Island was coming over the horizon. "That's home," he said.

As they flew closer, Scotty asked, "Is it actually an island? It looks to me as though it were connected with the main shore."

"It is, at low tide," Rick admitted. "The back side of the island is a tidal flat, all rocks. They're mostly under water at high tide."

The island was almost below now. Rick pointed out the house and laboratories, discreetly failing to mention the big rocket launcher in Pirate's Field; then he pointed to the neat farm buildings on the island's cultivated north side.

"That's where we get our vegetables and milk," he told Scotty. "The Huggins family runs the farm for us, on shares."

Scotty raised up in his seat and peered up over the nose. "I was wondering where you were going to land this thing. The strip between the sea and the trees?"

"That's right," Rick said. "Shall I land right side up for a change?"

"If you don't mind." Scotty grinned. "I've got more uses for this neck of mine later on." He watched Rick bank out to sea, losing altitude. "It looks like a wonderful place to live."

"It is," Rick agreed. He wanted to say more, to tell Scotty how much fun it was and what good times the family had together, but it was hard to talk about anything so personal and important.

He brought the Cub around in a smooth, 180-degree turn, lining up the nose with the grassy strip. The house flashed by and then they were over the grass. He held the plane off until it "sold out"; then he let it roll along to the place where his tie ropes were staked out.

"Home," he announced. "Here's the welcoming committee." He pointed to Dismal, who was coming through the orchard as fast as his short legs would move.

Scotty climbed out, laughing at the pup's ungainly way of running.

Diz barked happily at Rick, wagging his tail until his whole body vibrated. He paid no attention to Scotty until his young master said, "Say hello to Scotty, Dismal."

The dog walked over, nose outstretched to sniff Scotty's waiting hand. He sat down and examined the hand thoughtfully, while the marine waited.

"He's deciding," Rick said.

Dismal cocked his head, decided that Scotty was acceptable, barked once, and rolled over on his back, all four legs in the air.

"That's his trick," Rick explained. "The only one he knows. That means he likes you."

Scotty laughed. "A thoughtful dog with one trick," he said. "That's really something."

Rick led the way to the columned porch of the house. He was tempted to stop and show his newest gadget to Scotty, but he knew they should see his father at once.

Hartson Brant was in his office, hard at work on a mathematical problem. He rose as the boys entered.

"Did you get the tube, Rick?" His eyes on Scotty were curious.

"No, Dad." Before the scientist could ask questions, Scotty was introduced.

"Welcome to Spindrift," Hartson Brant said cordially. He shook Scotty's hand and motioned him to a chair. Then he faced his son. "Rick, I think you'd better explain that bump on your head."

He listened in silence as Rick told his story. Then he shook his head and said, "That was a foolish and dangerous thing to do, chasing those men, son. You had no right."

"But they were buying up all the triodes in Newark, Dad. I couldn't let them get away with that."

"I'm afraid you were a little overzealous, Rick." He put a hand on the boy's shoulder. "But I appreciate your loyalty, son. However, I'm sure your suspicions are unfounded. And you can't blame the men in the sedan for getting angry, can you? They probably were on some perfectly innocent errand."

"But they bought at least two dozen triodes, Dad. They couldn't use that many."

"I think they could," Hartson Brant said. "Suppose they were making a full-power pack for a high-power transmitter? Wouldn't they use a large bank of triodes then?"

"I guess so," Rick admitted. He decided to let the thing drop. There was a chance that his father was right.

Hartson Brant turned to Scotty. "Even if my son was mistaken, Scotty, I'm none the less grateful to you. You said you were just discharged from the marines?"

"That's right, sir."

"Do you have your discharge?"

Scotty produced a leather folder from inside his green blouse and handed it to the scientist.

Hartson Brant read the parchment carefully. "Tarawa, Saipan, Okinawa. You evidently saw a lot of action."

"Enough so that I don't want to see any more," Scotty said.

"I can understand that. According to your discharge, you enlisted at the age of seventeen."

"That's what it says, sir," Scotty nodded. He seemed suddenly ill at ease.

Rick cast a sharp look at his father.

Hartson Brant smiled. "That would make you just over twenty, and somehow I don't think you're that old. Let's have it, son. Were you underage when you enlisted?"

Scotty turned pink. "Yes, I was big for my age. The recruiting sergeant didn't ask too many questions."

"I had an idea it was something like that," Hartson Brant said, smiling. Then after a pause, "How would you like to work for me?"

Rick held his breath.

"I'd like nothing better, sir, but I don't know anything about science," Scotty said slowly.

"That's not necessary. I think we might use a guard until the experiment is over. At least you can keep inquisitive newspaper reporters away from the rocket launcher. The job is yours if you want it."

"Thank you, sir. I accept with pleasure."

"Fine. Rick will show you a room. Tomorrow we'll talk about a salary and some civilian clothes for you."

Rick grinned from ear to ear, delighted that Scotty would not have to continue on his lonely way to New York. He had taken a liking to the young marine on sight.

"We'll have to do without the triode until tomorrow, Rick," his father said. "It will be all right, I think. The new panel is almost assembled, so we haven't lost much time."

A voice asked, "Did I hear something about doing without the triode?"

They looked up as John Stringfellow came into the office. Rick introduced Scotty, whom the tall technician

greeted cordially, then explained, "I couldn't get a tube.
I tried a half-dozen places and they were sold out."

"Hmm. That's odd," Stringfellow commented. "Did
you try Royal Electronics?"

"No," Rick admitted.

"I'll see if they have any in stock," Stringfellow said.
He glanced at his watch. "Someone should still be
there."

He picked up the phone and asked for a Newark number. Rick heard him speak with Barby, then heard her
say, "Here's your party."

"This is Spindrift Island, Stringfellow speaking." He
gave the number of the tube and waited a moment
while someone at the other end made a quick check.
Presently he said, "Fine, we'd like three. Will you de-
liver them to the boat landing at Whiteside, first thing
in the morning? Thank you."

He smiled at Rick. "Easy enough. I'll run over in one
of the motorboats in the morning and pick them up."

Hartson Brant looked at his son as if to say, "See,
Rick? It wasn't a plot after all."

The boy turned red under his tan and said, "I'll show
Scotty to his room now."

Upstairs, Scotty looked around. "You mean this room
is all mine?"

"Sure. Is it all right?"

"All right?" Scotty put his hand in the middle of the

bed and tested the spring as though he couldn't believe
it was real. "After living in tents or barracks for so long,
it's like a corner of heaven."

"My room's right here through this connecting door.
The bath is down the hall. Come on, I'll get you clean
towels."

In a few moments they were cleaned up, only Rick's
bruise showing evidence of the fight. They went downstairs to the big dining room.

The Brants and the scientists had already gathered.
Rick introduced Scotty to the people he hadn't met, noting Barby's quick interest.

Throughout the meal Rick noticed Scotty's amazement at the good-natured banter that passed between
the dignified-looking scientists. "They only look formal,"
he told the marine, when they had finished dinner and
retired to their rooms. "They're really regular guys."

As they entered Rick's room, Scotty stopped short, his
glance taking in the weird assortment of gadgets.

"Come on in," Rick said. "I'll explain the place to
you."

"You'll have to. What is it? An electrical museum?"

"Brant Hall of Electronic Science," Rick replied, and
proceeded to show his new friend the arrangements he
had made for what he called "the simple, more comfortable life."

Above the radiator was an intricately wired alarm

clock. He set it and turned the hands ahead. As it went off, the windows slid shut, the heat lever on the radiator flew into the "on" position, and the radio turned on.

Scotty looked impressed.

"That's nothing," Rick said. "Sit down in that chair."

He was proudest of all of the old leather chair he had rigged up. Along one arm was a row of buttons. The first controlled the reading lamp, a motor rheostat giving just the amount of light required for any purpose. The second turned on the radio, the third controlled the volume, the fourth gave a choice of five stations, depending on how many times it was depressed.

"Push the fifth one," Rick invited with a grin.

Scotty gave it a wary push. The back of the chair flopped down and a footrest shot into position. He recovered his balance with an effort and found that the adjustment was perfect for reading in a stretched-out position.

Rick grinned at Scotty's look of awe. "This is my workbench over here," he said. He pushed a catch and a wall shelf opened. It revealed a neat bench, complete with soldering irons, coils of wire, jars of switches, and other parts. On one end was a small wooden box.

Rick picked it up. "This is something I'm working on now."

Scotty examined it. "Looks like the spark coil off an old model T Ford.

"That's just what it is. I want to rig it up so I can carry it on my belt with a couple of batteries. Then, when I turn on the juice and touch something— Wow!"

Scotty scratched his head. "What's the idea? You don't go around giving people shocks just for fun, do you?"

"Sometimes," Rick said. "The scientists get playful now and then. A few days ago Professor Zircon saw me come into the lab, so he charged a Leyden jar—that's a jar that stores electricity. He left it where I'd be sure to pick it up. It's a bad habit I have, always handling things. I grabbed the Leyden jar and zowie! I let out a yelp that could be heard in Europe. So I'm working on something to get back at the prof."

"Nice place." Scotty grinned. "I'd better wear rubber soles for insulation with all this electricity around." He hesitated. "Want to tell me what's happening here? I'm so curious I could bust a seam."

Rick began tinkering with the spark coil. He could always talk better when his hands were busy.

"Well," he began, "I guess the best place to start is at the beginning."

Scotty made himself comfortable in the gadget-controlled armchair. "It usually is," he agreed.

"Before the war," Rick went on, "Dad worked at the university as professor of physics. There wasn't any laboratory here then, except for a little one where Dad tinkered with things. Then the government asked him to take over one phase of radar development."

"Radar?" Scotty gave a low whistle. "I've seen it work, Is that something!"

"Anyway they needed labs, so the government put up the money and built this one, and they asked Dad to get a staff together. They worked all during the war. The scientists decided that they made a swell team. They wanted to stay together after the war, but the government decided to tear down the lab. The scientists were sick about it, but there wasn't anything they could do. Then along came old John Stoneridge."

"The millionaire?"

"That's the one. He's over eighty, you know. He decided to parcel out some of his millions. He had a grant of two million dollars set up for the electrical sciences, only he put a few strings on it."

Scotty was sitting upright. "What kind of strings?"

"The two million will be given to the group of scientists making the most important contribution to their special field within a single year. A year isn't much time for a really big development, you know. But Dad and the others decided to make a try for it, anyway. They pooled all the money they had, borrowed more, and then they went to work. That was in July, last year."

"Then the year is almost up."

Rick nodded. "A little less than a week to go."

"But what's the thing they're working on?"

"A rocket to the moon."

Scotty sank back in the armchair and stared.

"It's big," Rick said. "It's the biggest thing since the atom bomb, I guess. And we're almost ready. Dad and the others are assembling the control units now. The rocket will be controlled by radar."

"But how will you know where it is once it takes off?" Scotty objected.

"The radar scopes will tell us. Besides, there will be about a ton of explosive in the nose. When it hits the moon, there will be a blast big enough to be seen by telescope."

"How about the fuel?" Scotty still looked disbelieving.

"That was a big problem," Rick admitted. "Then Dr. Wisecarver, one of the scientists, developed a new fuel that's powerful enough to do the trick. He got some of the radioactive stuff left over from atom-bomb manufacture and worked it out with that."

"You said about a dozen scientists. I've only met three."

"The others are taking a vacation. Their part is done, and they're not needed now. They'll all be back in a few days, to be here when the rocket goes off. The place will be overrun with scientists, reporters, and gosh knows who else."

"I've really stepped into big doings," Scotty said.

"Look. What happens if the thing doesn't work?"

"It has to," Rick declared flatly. "It just *has* to. Dad says it will, and so do the others."

"But if it doesn't?" Scotty persisted.

"Then," Rick said slowly, "the lab will be torn down, and the swellest, most wonderful gang of people in the world will have to break up and go back to teaching and things like that. But it can't miss, Scotty! You wait and see."

"If your dad and the others could help develop radar, they can do this. I'm convinced." Scotty rumpled his black hair thoughtfully. "Look, Rick. I saw your face when you were talking to your father. You think those men were buying up the tubes to keep you from getting one, don't you?"

"Yes."

"But how did they know you were going to Newark to get a tube?"

"I'd like to know," Rick replied soberly.

Scotty walked to the window. "It's raining," he said. "Say, is that the lab over in back of the orchard?"

"That's right."

"There's a light on in there."

"Probably Dad or one of the others working on the control panel. Want to go over? I can show you through the lab."

"And how! I want to see this moon rocket."

They went downstairs and out into the warm darkness of the orchard. The rain was letting up, so they didn't need coats.

"Someone's in the radiation room," Rick said. His voice was loud in the darkness.

As he spoke, the light went out. Then they heard a door slam, followed by the sound of running feet.

"Someone's running away from there!" Scotty exclaimed. He pulled a pencil flashlight from his pocket and shot the beam through the trees. For an instant, the moving light shone squarely into Rick's eyes, blinding him.

"Where? I can't see." Rick shielded his eyes and tried to catch a glimpse of the figure. "Where did he go?"

"Come on." Scotty picked his way through the orchard to where the figure had vanished. There was no sign of anyone.

"Down this path is the shortest way."

Rick, his night vision regained, struck off through the trees to where the dark bulk of the lab was dimly visible.

Something white flickered in the air and swerved into full sight. It was luminous, and it fluttered through the air like a blind ghost. It fell to the ground a short distance away, jerked feebly, and then lay still.

"A ghost," Scotty breathed.

"The ghost of a bird, then," Rick retorted, but the words hid his own sudden fright.

They hurried to where the thing glowed against the ground in front of the laboratory. It stirred weakly, as though trying to rise again.

"The flashlight," Rick said. Then, as Scotty shot the beam down, a horrified chill flashed through him.

"A bat!" Scotty exclaimed. "Look at it!"

Rick bent low over the luminous body and the chill turned his blood to ice.

He let out a hoarse cry.

"Dad! Come quickly! Dad!"

He took the light from Scotty's hand and shot it toward the house, blinking the beam off and on.

"What is it?" Scotty asked. "What's the matter?"

"Look at it." Rick choked. "The skin is . . . is melting right off. Scotty, the radiation shields are down!"

CHAPTER V

Trouble on Spindrift Island

Lights flashed on all over the house and there were shouts as people rushed across the orchard to where the boys stood.

"Rick, where are you?" Hartson Brant called.

"Here, Dad, in front of the radiation-room door."

The scientist hurried to their side, followed by other pajama-clad figures.

"The shields are down," Rick told them, pointing to the bat.

Scotty was the first to break the spell the glowing bat held over the group. "I'll take a look inside," he said, and started for the door.

Rick and Hartson Brant grabbed him together.

"You wouldn't last ten seconds in there," Rick said urgently. "See that bat?"

"Get the antiradiation suits," Hartson Brant directed. John Stringfellow hurried toward the storeroom, while the others went to the main door of the laboratory.

"What's it all about?" Scotty asked, bewildered.

"Gamma rays," Rick said. "The electron gun is in there, bombarding that radioactive pile of stuff I told you about. The combined rays are deadly. The lead shields that protect the operators must have fallen."

"But how could they fall?"

"I don't know," Rick answered. "But if the bat hadn't flown in and warned us . . . Well, we wouldn't have gone under so fast, but we'd have died in a few days."

They stood aside as Hartson Brant and John String-fellow hurried to the radiation-room door. They were dressed in strange suits of gray metal cloth and wore helmets of the same material on their heads. Their faces were nearly invisible behind thick, leaded glass. Completely covered by the odd outfits, they looked like men from another planet.

"Lead cloth," Rick explained, "to protect them from the rays while they put the shields back up."

The two curiously dressed men vanished into the inner room and the others waited in silence. They were back in a few moments, stripping off the radiation suits. No one spoke a word as they waited for Hartson Brant to break the silence.

The scientist's eyes went from face to face as his helmet came off and he stepped out of the cumbersome suit. Finally he spoke:

"Who was in the lab tonight?"

There was no answer.

"If the shields were dropped by accident, don't be afraid to speak up."

Rick took a deep breath and said, "I don't think it was an accident, Dad."

He felt all eyes on him. "Scotty and I saw a light in the lab," he went on, "and when we came to see what it was, this door was open and a man ran through the orchard."

"And if the bat hadn't warned you," Hartson Brant said grimly, "you might have gone right into the radiation room."

The boys nodded.

"Then whoever dropped those shields would have been guilty of murder!"

"Oh, no!" John Stringfellow gasped.

"What would you call it?" Hartson Brant asked. It was plain that he was making an effort at calmness.

Stringfellow shuddered. "Who would plan such a horrible thing?"

"And why?" Hobart Zircon's gruff voice added.

No one had an answer.

"Well, someone did drop the shields," Rick said at last. "We saw him leaving the lab."

"That's just it," Zircon boomed. "Did you actually see a man?"

"Scotty did." Rick looked at his friend.

"Yes, sir," Scotty said definitely. "I caught just a glimpse of him; then he vanished."

Julius Weiss spoke up tartly. "First you saw him; then you didn't. The light was poor, was it not? Perhaps you really saw nothing."

"Scotty saw him," Rick said flatly. "And I heard him slam the door."

"Well, I was in my room—" Zircon stopped quickly, aware that every eye was on him.

"No one has accused you," Hartson Brant said. "But as long as you say you can account for yourself, how about the rest of us?"

"I was also in my room," Julius Weiss said hurriedly. "And I thought I heard Hobart moving around next door."

The two men looked at each other and nodded.

"I was reading in my quarters," Stringfellow said.

"And I was in my room asleep," said Hartson Brant.

"Then the only ones up at the time were these two," Hobart Zircon declared, pointing a finger at Rick and Scotty.

"And we don't know this new boy very well," Julius Weiss cut in.

Scotty reddened at the insinuation. "I tell you I saw a man," he insisted defensively. "Rick was with me every minute."

"Just a moment," Hartson Brant interrupted. "There

is no need to throw accusations at each other. I see no reason for believing the prowler was one of us. Someone could very well have reached the island from the mainland."

"If there was such a person," Weiss said stubbornly.

"That's quite enough," Mr. Brant said coldly. "Prowler or not, I'm going to put a guard in the laboratory tonight. We can do some investigating tomorrow. Hobart, will you please stand watch on this side? Scotty will watch on the other side."

Zircon nodded agreement.

"The rest of us will return to the house," Hartson Brant added. "Scotty, before you begin, please come with me."

He led the way toward the house, all but Zircon following. One by one they turned off to their own rooms until only Rick and Scotty were left with the scientist. In his bedroom, he opened a bureau drawer and drew forth a black object.

Rick's eyes widened as his father said, "Take this, Scotty. I think you know how to use it."

Scotty took the service pistol, a .45 automatic. He nodded silently.

"Dad," Rick pleaded, "what do you really think?"

Hartson Brant looked suddenly old and tired. "All these strange accidents, and now this . . . I'm afraid someone is trying to interfere with our experiment."

Rick started to speak, but his father held up his hand. "We'll talk about it in the morning. Go to bed now."

The boys left the room and Hartson Brant closed the door behind them.

"When I left the marines I thought I'd never have to stand watch again," Scotty remarked. "But here goes." He tucked the pistol into his belt and went down the hall.

Rick looked after his vanishing figure and shook his head. In the last few weeks, a shadow had drifted over Spindrift Island.

CHAPTER VI

The Loosened Clasp

RICK awoke with a rapid buzzing in his ears. For a moment he lay still, trying to fathom the noise; then he realized someone was ringing the switchboard for an outside line.

He swept off the covers and dressed rapidly. Through the open door he heard his father's voice.

"Barby, where are you? Connect me with an outside line, please."

Rick went into the hall as his sister hurried downstairs to the switchboard. His father was phoning from his own room.

"Come in, Rick," he said when his son appeared at the door. Then, "Operator? State Police Headquarters, please."

Rick tensed. Like all boys his age, he had a wholesome respect for the police. It was an uncomfortable feeling to know that their help was needed on Spindrift Island.

"Lieutenant Slocum? This is Hartson Brant. Yes, on Spindrift Island."

Rick listened as his father outlined the events of the night before.

"Is he coming?" he asked when his father hung up.

"Yes, he'll be here in an hour."

"You're going to tell him everything, aren't you, Dad? About the man we saw and all?"

Hartson Brant chose a necktie and put it on. "I'm afraid I won't be here, son. I have an appointment in New York with the Stoneridge people. It can't be canceled. I'm putting John Stringfellow in charge."

Rick felt disappointment at the news, but he realized the trip was important if it was about the grant. "I'll go see if Scotty wants breakfast," he said. "I'll see you before you go, Dad."

Hartson Brant was finishing breakfast when Rick returned with a famished Scotty. As the boys sat down, he rose and took his small traveling bag.

"I'll be back as soon as I can," he told them. "Meanwhile, keep your eyes open, both of you. But stay out of trouble." He left the house and went toward the boat landing.

Barby joined them at the breakfast table. Her eyes, on Scotty, were solicitous. "Aren't you tired, after staying up all night?"

"Not at all," Scotty assured her. "Just hungry. I'm used to standing watches."

"Good," Rick said. "Then maybe you'd like to take a little excursion."

"Soon as I finish this," Scotty answered, reaching for one of Mrs. Brant's fluffy biscuits.

Barby spread her biscuit liberally with butter, glancing at Rick to see if he was watching.

"Mustn't," he said, grinning. "You'll never get to Hollywood eating a pound of butter at every meal."

"You eat it, and it doesn't keep you from playing detective," she said defiantly. "Anyway, who wants to go to Hollywood?"

"You," Rick teased.

"Not any more," Barby said comfortably. "I've decided to be a girl marine." The look she gave Scotty was one of pure hero worship.

Rick tried to look blank. "Where do you get that detective stuff?"

"On the telephone. I listened when Dad was telephoning."

Rick shook his head. "Shameless," he said. "Imagine, Scotty, my little sister turns out to be an eavesdropper!"

"I'm not so little," she said quickly. "I guess I'm old enough to go on that excursion with you."

Rick looked at Scotty. He seemed amused at the conversation. He wouldn't mind if Barby went along.

"I guess you're old enough," he agreed. "Come on."

The three rose from the table and went out of doors, where Dismal greeted them happily and tumbled along scatter-footed in the lead.

They headed toward Pirate's Field. Barby threw a stick for Dismal to retrieve, but the shaggy pup couldn't locate it in the grass, and she ran off to help him.

Scotty stepped quickly to Rick's side. "There's a funny look on your face," he said. "What's on your mind?"

It was hard to put the thought in words. "Maybe I'm wrong," Rick said hesitantly. "I hope I am. But I'm beginning to believe that if anyone is trying to wreck the experiment, he has a helper here on the island."

Scotty's eyes opened wide. "That's plenty serious. Have you said anything to your father?"

"My gosh, no! Dad has known tnese men for years. He'd think I had gone crazy."

"But what makes you think so?"

Rick stopped walking. "Well, we've had a lot of trouble that seemed accidental. It would take an inside man to make those things look like accidents. Then, last night, the shields were dropped. It would take someone who knew what he was doing to fool around the radiation chamber without getting burned. And two of the men tried hard to convince us we didn't see any prowler."

"Zircon?"

"And Weiss."

"That's pretty slim evidence." Scotty scratched his head. "The worst part of it is, if you're right we can't do anything about it until the traitor makes his next move."

They heard Barby calling to them and looked up to see her standing before a tall, angular framework covered with canvas.

"She wants to show you the rocket launcher," Rick said.

As they arrived at Barby's side, Scotty whistled at the height of the great frame. "This is certainly no Fourth-of-July rocket you folks are going to shoot off!"

"It will be the largest and most powerful rocket ever launched from the earth," Rick said seriously.

Barby lifted a corner of the canvas and peeked under it.

"Nuhnuh," Rick cautioned. "Mustn't touch."

Barby dropped the canvas as though it were red-hot. "Oh, I know what it looks like," she said pertly.

"All right, little sister," Rick invited, "tell us how it works."

"Well, it's a—I mean, there's a big whatchamacallit, a slide, sort of, for the rocket to sit in."

"She means a cradle." Rick grinned.

"Yes. And right down here"—she pointed to the base of the tall frame—"is a thingamajig that starts the rocket."

"She means a detonating chamber," Rick explained.

Barby turned pink. "Well, you're so smart! You tell it."

Scotty smiled. "It shouldn't be hard to be a scientist. Why, everyone knows what thingamajigs and whatchamacallits are."

Barby looked embarrassed but she laughed.

Rick came to her rescue. "Those are as good names as any, I guess. The instruments are all specially made for radar control. They didn't have any names until the scientists figured out what to call them."

"What are these instruments supposed to do?"

"They'll be set to transmit back to Spindrift. Dope about temperature and rays and solar radiation—all kinds of stuff. They'll tell us what outer space is like."

He held the canvas aside so Scotty could see the steel framework which stretched up under the cover. Dismal poked an inquisitive nose under the canvas and Rick pulled him back.

Scotty shook his head. "Whoever would have believed we'd be hitting the moon with rockets someday?" he marveled.

"That someday is only a few days away now," Rick said. He added softly, "I hope."

"You hope?" Barby asked. "Why, Daddy has it definitely scheduled. Why are you acting so funny?"

Rick smiled quickly. "Don't be inquisitive," he said

good-naturedly. Suddenly the smile vanished. "Say, look!" He pointed toward the lab.

A blue-serge figure was talking to John Stringfellow before the laboratory door.

"Must be your police—" Scotty stopped. "Must be the man they were expecting," he finished.

"A policeman," Barby said. "I listened in when Daddy called."

Rick nodded. "We'll see you later, Barby."

The two boys hurried off toward the lab. When they arrived, John Stringfellow and the detective were just entering the room that housed the electron gun.

"So this is what caused all the trouble last night," they heard the detective say. He was a hard-muscled man with glinting, gray eyes.

"This is the electron gun, yes," John Stringfellow was saying. He looked up as the boys walked in. "Oh, and this is Hartson Brant's son, Rick . . . and his friend, Scotty."

"You're the two boys who came out and found this thing in a mess, eh?" the detective said.

"That's right," Rick answered. "And just as we came out—"

John Stringfellow interrupted him. "A bat had flown into the path of the deadly rays and was completely irradiated. But we can't understand how the shields could have fallen."

"What shields?" the detective asked, glancing at the strange mechanism.

John Stringfellow pointed to two wide, lead panels that housed the electron gun. "These," he said. "They protect the workers from the rays."

The detective squatted to look at the panels. His eyes traveled the length of them and suddenly stopped at the bar-type clasp that held the doorlike shields tight against the face of the opening.

"What's this?" he inquired.

The two boys bent low to look. "The clasp! It's broken!" Rick exclaimed in amazement.

"Yes," the detective said, straightening up. "Did that happen when the shields were dropped last night?"

"I was just going to say," Stringfellow cut in. "I seem to remember— This is very embarrassing . . . but I seem to remember the clasp being loose."

At that moment, footsteps were heard behind them. Hobart Zircon walked into the room.

"Oh, Hobart," Stringfellow said. "Didn't you mention something to me about this clasp being loose last night?"

The huge scientist bent to look. "I— Yes, there was something said about it. I thought *you* had told *me* about it."

"No," the lean scientist insisted, turning toward the detective. "Zircon told me this was loose. I intended to see about it, but I was busy, and forgot."

"Then these lead shields could have fallen down because the clasp was loose, right?" the detective asked.

"Yes, I'm afraid they could have," Stringfellow answered.

The detective heaved a disgusted sigh and rose. "It seems pretty apparent to me that that is just what happened. The loose clasp caused all your trouble."

"But what about the man we saw?" Rick asked suddenly.

"Man? What man?" the detective questioned.

"These boys claim to have seen a man running away from here last night," Zircon interrupted. "But we came to the conclusion that in their excitement they imagined they had seen someone."

"Oh, great!" the detective fumed. "I'm called all the way out here because a piece of equipment has a loose clasp, and a couple of kids start seeing things!" He snorted disdainfully, "Scientists!" Then he walked out.

Rick and Scotty walked to the door through which the irate detective had vanished.

"Well, that was short and sweet," Scotty said. "It was an accident!"

"Are you kidding?" Rick asked sharply.

Scotty grinned. "Why, the detective couldn't be *wrong*, could he?"

"Not only *could*. He *was*," Rick said. "And do you know why?"

Scotty nodded his head. "I'm not dumb," he said. "Zircon claims that the clasp on the shields was on the blink last night. He told Stringfellow about it, but Stringfellow didn't see it. Zircon could have knocked it off last night so it would look like an accident when it was found this morning," Scotty continued. "Or he could have smashed the clasp while we were at breakfast."

"That's exactly the way it looks to me," Rick said. "I think Hobart Zircon may be the man we've got to watch!"

CHAPTER VII

The Sign on the Barn

"WHAT are you going to do about Zircon?" Scotty asked.

"There's little we can do except keep an eye on him, and wait for his next move," Rick answered. "I wish Dad were here."

Scotty was deep in thought. Suddenly he said, "Rick, there's a question that hasn't been answered. Why would anyone want to wreck this experiment?"

"I think it has something to do with the Stoneridge grant. Remember, it's worth two million dollars."

"That's reason enough, right there," Scotty declared.

"But the traitor couldn't work this thing alone," Rick mused. "I wonder— Do you suppose those men in the sedan could be mixed up in it?"

"Could be," Scotty said thoughtfully. "But we couldn't prove it."

"If the man we saw last night was the traitor," Rick went on, "he would not have left the island. Right?"

"No, he probably circled and got back in the house while all the excitement was going on," Scotty agreed.

"And don't forget, it rained last night," Rick said excitedly. "Why wouldn't there be tracks?"

Scotty snapped his fingers. "By golly, you're right. Let's go look!"

The boys hurried to the laboratory door. The graveled path in front of the entrance was trodden by many feet and useless for tracking purposes, but just beyond the path, at the edge of the orchard, Rick stopped.

"Here! Look, Scotty!"

There in the still damp ground was a muddy footprint.

"And big too," Rick added significantly, looking toward Zircon's huge bulk through the lab window.

"Here's another one," Scotty called from a few feet beyond.

Rick hurried to his side, and inch by inch they covered the orchard. A few times they thought the trail had been lost, but each time, one of them would find a heelprint or the impression of a toe in the soft earth. The trail led them deep into the woods of the island and then out on a winding path.

"This leads to the tidal flats," Rick said. "And look!"

There, plainly engraved in the soft earth of the path, were clear footprints.

They followed the trail at a slow trot. Suddenly Rick

stopped dead. The path changed from dirt to solid rock. At that point the trail forked. Another path branched off to the left.

"Where does this one go?" Scotty asked.

"It circles around back to the house and lab," Rick answered.

"And this one?" Scotty indicated the path that continued straight on across the rocks.

"To the tidal flats," Rick told him. "And he could have gone either way, because both paths are rocky."

"Oh, fine!" Scotty said disgustedly. "Where does that leave us?"

"Well, if it was the traitor we saw last night, he'd have taken the left path back to the house. If it was someone from the mainland, he'd have gone straight to the tidal flats. Let's go have a look there."

Scotty had not yet seen the back end of Spindrift Island. As they walked out into a rocky clearing that fell away in a short but sheer drop to the rock-strewn tidal flats below, he gasped.

"What a view!" he exclaimed. "You can see half of New Jersey."

Rick looked out across the rock-studded water to the endless stretch of alternate woods and patched farm land that lay in every direction in the clear July sunlight. Directly across from the bluff were deep woods.

"We didn't come for the view," he said. "This is the only spot where a prowler could get on and off the island. I wonder if he did?"

Scotty stared at the rocky ledge. "It would be impossible to tell now."

"When the tide is low, it would be easy to cross," Rick commented. "Right now it's almost high, but still possible. And last night, when we saw that man, the tide was high."

"Well, what do we do now?"

Rick shook his head slowly. "We're stopped right here. I guess all we can accomplish now is to look at the view."

Scotty shaded his eyes and scanned the mainland. "Look," he said. "You can even read the sign on top of that barn over there, and it must be a mile away."

"You can read it, not me," Rick answered with a grin. "You're the boy with the jungle eyes; and it's easily two miles away."

"I can read it all right," Scotty said. "It says . . . 'Drink . . . White . . . Cream.'"

Rick jeered. "I thought you were the boy with the X-ray eyes. That sign says 'Smoke White Cream.' I know, because we flew over it yesterday."

Scotty squinted again. "Nope. It says 'Drink.' Not 'Smoke.' I'm positive, Rick."

Rick looked thoughtfully at his pal, then turned and stared in the direction of the barn, shading his eyes with his hands.

"Golly, you're right, Scotty!" he exclaimed as he turned around. "Now what do you suppose that means?" he asked.

"Means?" Scotty looked puzzled. "Look, you're getting so jumpy you think everything is connected with this business on the island."

"Yes, I guess you're right," Rick agreed. "It's probably my memory. But I could have sworn—" He took another look at the sign on the barn and shook his head. "Okay. Let's go."

They turned and headed back toward the path to the house. Suddenly Scotty stopped, grabbing Rick's arm. "Down!" he whispered hoarsely.

The two boys dropped flat and Rick looked at Scotty. "What's up?" he whispered.

Scotty pointed. "Watch the edge of the cliff—at the tidal flats," he said.

Rick stared at the ledge toward which Scotty was pointing. For a moment the dazzling sunlight blinded him, but suddenly his heart skipped.

Reaching over the edge of the cliff was a hand!

CHAPTER VIII

A Traitor on the Island?

THE two boys hugged the rocks as the hand clutched for a firmer hold on the edge of the cliff. Slowly the hand was joined by an arm, then a shoulder and finally a head. A battered felt hat, pulled low over the face, covered the head. The boys saw the stranger look quickly about, obviously worried about detection.

"It'd take one kick to knock him back down," Scotty whispered.

Rick took his arm. "No, let him get up first."

The man hauled himself up and stood erect near the edge of the cliff. Then he started running straight toward the path. The boys were hidden by low bushes and the intruder didn't see them.

The man bent low, glancing back over his shoulder as he ran. Suddenly he jerked his head up and fear leaped into his eyes.

Scotty flew through the air directly at him. Over on his back the stranger went, swinging wildly. Scotty's fist flashed back and in the tenth of a second it took to start it toward the intruder's jaw Rick yelled, "No, Scotty!"

Scotty's fist held in midair.

Rick leaped to his side and grabbed his arm. "No," he commanded. "I know him."

The prostrate figure rolled over with a weak grin. "Hello, Rick," he said.

"Jerry Webster," Rick said sternly. "What are you doing here?"

"I was looking for a story for the *Morning Record*. But your friend interrupted me."

The young reporter got to his feet and brushed the dirt from his flashy sports coat. Then he tenderly dusted his battered felt hat.

"You might have been hurt, you idiot," Rick said. "What's the big idea?"

"My paper assigned me to cover the rocket," Jerry answered. "It's the first real assignment I've had. So I thought I'd sneak over and get a little dope for an advance story." He rubbed his jaw. "I had no idea you were so jealous of your little secrets."

"The best thing you can do is turn right around and go back to the mainland," Rick told him. "We're having troubles enough."

"Troubles?" An eager look, like a hound's on the scent, came into the reporter's face. "What kind of trouble? Remember, in my business bad news makes good news."

"You'll get the whole story from Dad when the time comes," Rick promised. "But don't try to get any information this way again."

"Okay," Jerry said. "I can take a hint." He grinned and turned swiftly. In a moment he vanished back over the cliff.

Rick and Scotty looked at each other.

"If he could get across those flats so easily, why couldn't someone else?" Scotty demanded.

"They could," Rick agreed. "Jerry didn't allow himself much margin, though. The tide goes out very early in the morning. It's almost high tide now. I think we'd better keep an eye on this part of the island." He took another look at the distant barn. "More stuff to confuse a fellow," he said soberly.

They went back along the path and in a few minutes reached the clearing near the laboratory.

Rick saw his mother talking to John Stringfellow. She waved to him and he hurried to her side.

"Your father called from New York," she said. "He won't be able to get back for two or three days."

Rick's heart sank.

"Don't be disappointed." Stringfellow smiled. "We

can take care of things that long. Certainly nothing more should happen in that short time."

"Is the work going on?" Rick asked.

"We're not doing much until your father returns. We'll need him for the final assembly and instrument calibration. The rest of us know very little about that."

"I guess there's nothing to do but wait," Rick concluded. He yawned suddenly. "What do you say we rest awhile, Scotty?"

They went upstairs to Rick's room and Scotty flopped at full length on the bed.

"Let's hope we have a little peace for a while," Scotty said wearily. "I'm dead."

"That's the trouble," Rick said, dropping into a chair. "We can only hope. The traitor knows we have to wait for his next move. He's probably planning it right now."

He turned over the recent events in his mind, searching for some connecting thread, something that would tie them together. There was only one thing that seemed to show a pattern.

He spoke his thoughts aloud. "I don't think anyone is trying to wreck the experiment entirely. They could have done that with a fire, or an explosion. I think they're only trying to delay us."

Scotty came out of his doze. "It makes sense," he agreed.

"What's more," Rick went on, "they tried to make us think all the accidents were plain bad luck. That's why it was usually something that could be blamed on defective equipment. That relay might have been tampered with, and it would have been easy to cause an overload that would burn things out. But why would they want to slow us down? I don't get it."

"It beats me," Scotty said.

Both boys jumped as a rapping sounded at the door. In a second Rick was on his feet, opening it. Julius Weiss stood there blinking at him.

The little scientist looked up and down the hall as though to make sure no one was watching, then stepped into the room and closed the door.

"I must see you," he said.

Weiss looked frightened.

"What is it, sir?" Rick asked.

The scientist took a deep breath and looked from one boy to the other. "Boys," he said, "I'm beginning to agree with you."

"About what?" Rick asked.

"About there being something peculiar going on. Now I find myself the victim!"

Instantly the boys were alert.

The scientist sat down at Rick's invitation, but he perched on the edge of his chair and rubbed his hands nervously. "I became suspicious last night," he went on. "It seemed to me that someone had been in my room, although nothing was disturbed. So I decided to set a trap. I put a piece of Scotch tape across the crack between the drawer and the leg of my desk. I have a number of important papers there. I knew that if the drawer were pulled open, the tape would be torn. It was only a small piece. When I looked this morning, the tape was unstuck. I think that someone was looking at the rocket-fuel formula!"

For an instant Rick was hopeful that it might be a tangible clue; then he shook his head. "I'm afraid it doesn't mean anything, sir. It rained last night, and Scotch tape loses its sticky qualities in wet weather. The tape probably came unstuck by itself."

Julius Weiss slumped in his chair. "I didn't think of that," he said. "You're right, of course. Then I have no proof that my desk was disturbed."

"I'm afraid not, sir."

"I was so sure." Weiss stood up. "But I must have been wrong, of course. These things must be accidents after all." He nodded to the boys and left the room.

Rick looked at Scotty. "Funny. Wouldn't you think that a wizard like Professor Weiss could think up something smarter than that?"

"Maybe," Scotty said. "What are you getting at?"

"I don't think he put the tape on his desk at all," Rick

declared. "I think it was just something he dreamed up to throw suspicion from himself."

Scotty groaned. "Suppose you're right? That makes it a bigger mess than ever. Who's your traitor? Weiss? You haven't anything but suspicions about him. No, Rick, it doesn't stand up. The traitor could still be any scientist on the island."

CHAPTER IX

The Black Plane Means Business

IT WAS impossible to stay put with so much tension in the air. Rick and Scotty wandered over to the laboratory and were joined by Dismal, who scampered ahead of them and got underfoot as they walked about, trying to look innocent.

Once Zircon growled at Dismal, who, realizing that he didn't belong in the sacred precincts of the lab, ran frantically to Rick for moral support.

In the inner workshop they came across Stringfellow. He was looking at a leather case that rested on top of a bookshelf. As the boys came up to him, he smiled and said, "I'd certainly like to own these."

Rick recognized them as expensive binoculars of a German make.

"Even the service binoculars weren't as good as those," Scotty said admiringly.

Stringfellow slipped them back into the case. "They

belong to Professor Weiss," he explained. "He doesn't like anyone to handle them. In fact, I didn't even know he had them until he brought them down here for something."

The three walked back to the central room, chatting amiably. As they entered the radar transmitter section, they saw Julius Weiss bending over an open panel in the rack.

He looked up, surprised, as they entered, and stammered, "Here's another part of the panel that burned out. I just discovered it."

Stringfellow bent low and looked at the coil in Weiss's hands. "It certainly is burned out," he said. "And we haven't another of these on hand."

"I can run over to Newark and get another," Rick offered quickly.

"All right," Stringfellow agreed. "I think your mother wants some groceries, too, so you can stop at Whiteside on the same trip."

"I'll get my jacket and see what Mother wants," Rick said. "Come on, Scotty."

As they walked to the house, Rick anticipated his friend's question. "No, I don't think there was anything treacherous about the coil. I think it was burned out with the rest of the panel."

Scotty grinned. "I'm getting to be as suspicious as you are."

After getting the grocery list from his mother, Rick went to the air strip.

"There's Stringfellow," Scotty said.

The thin scientist was waiting at the plane. "Just in case you didn't know the exact specifications, I wrote them down for you," he said, handing the sheet of paper to Rick.

Rick thanked the scientist and climbed into the plane while Scotty pulled the prop through. He leaped in beside Rick and in a moment they were in the air, heading for Whiteside.

Far below, the farm lands of New Jersey baked in the July sun. Suddenly Scotty pointed ahead and to the left. "Look, there's the barn. It says 'Drink,' all right."

Rick looked down at it. "I'll bet anything that sign said 'Smoke' yesterday," he said. He pointed to the gray car he had seen just to the left of the barn. "It must have been changed. But why?"

"It's their sign; they can change it if they like," Scotty said grinning.

"Yes, but why from 'Smoke' to 'Drink'? It doesn't make sense. And what is 'White Cream,' anyway?"

"Maybe a soft drink, maybe a cigar," Scotty shrugged. "Maybe both. Don't ask me; I'm as confused as you are."

The Whiteside Airport was under their wings now. Rick banked into the wind and landed. They rolled up to his usual parking place next to the hangar.

Mac trotted up. "Gas?" he asked.

"Right. Where's Gus?"

"Inside." The mechanic reached for the gas hose as the boys walked into the hangar.

Gus was bent over the engine of a small plane that had been torn down for repair.

"Well, if it isn't one of the Wright Brothers!" was Rick's greeting.

Gus wiped his face and scowled good-naturedly. "Hello, fly-boy. Where to this time?"

"A little errand, soon as your hired hand fills the Cub."

Gus looked out to where Mac was filling the tank. "He really goes for that baby of yours. He was giving it the once-over yesterday."

"Sure," Rick jibed. "After the broken-down kites you people see all day, it must be nice to have a real airplane around." He walked back to the plane with Scotty. Mac had finished gassing it up and was standing near the tail.

"Like it, Mac?" Rick asked.

Mac jerked his head up. "Yeah, sure do. Wish I had one." He turned and began stowing the gas hose.

"Let's go, Scotty." Rick started to climb into the cabin, but Scotty stopped him.

"Your tail door is open again," he said.

The tail inspection port was slightly open. Rick went back and closed it, turning the catch with his pocketknife. "It must be loose somewhere," he remarked. "I'll fix it when we get home."

Scotty hung back as he climbed into the Cub. Rick looked at him questioningly.

"I just remembered," Scotty said. "I'm supposed to be a guard. I ought to be guarding instead of joy riding. Why don't I pick up the groceries? I'll get the stuff and phone Barby to pick me up in one of the boats. Then I'll go home and sleep for a while before I go on watch."

It was a sensible suggestion. "See you at home, then," Rick said.

Gus walked from the hangar as they spoke. "Say, Mac didn't get into your hair, did he? I took him up on leaving that inspection port open and he said he never touched it. I saw you close it again just now. I'll tell him to lay off touching things that aren't his."

"Maybe he's trying to hunt up repair jobs for you." Rick grinned. "Turn it over, will you, Gus?"

The engine roared into life. Rick waved to Scotty and rolled down the strip for the take-off.

Once in the air, he pushed the little plane to slightly better than normal cruising speed. It wasn't long before the Newark Airport came in sight. He landed and took a taxi to Cotter's, where he made his purchase.

"Well, one good thing, they don't seem to use the same tricks twice," Rick mused. "At least I could get the part."

He hurried back to the airport, happy that he was making good time. After a short wait for instructions from the Newark tower, he was again in the air, flying toward Spindrift. The railroad below passed from the crowded Newark district into flat farm lands. Rick glanced around at the scene rolling underneath the Cub's sturdy wings. Off to the east, he caught a glimpse of ocean and swung toward it. His altimeter read three thousand feet.

Then something flashed past the corner of his eye. He turned just as a black biplane shot underneath him.

Rick banked away. "Crazy," he muttered. "Does he want the whole sky to himself?"

The black plane was pulling up in a wild climb a thousand feet away. It was a strange model, with retractable landing gear, variable pitch propeller, and all the latest gadgets. Rick had often yearned for something like it, but that class of plane was surely in the neighborhood of twenty thousand dollars. He noticed the airplane registration number as it climbed and made a mental note of it.

"He must feel good," Rick said admiringly. "He wants to play."

The pilot had leveled off. Now he was doing snap rolls. As he came out of one, he pulled the biplane up in a tight vertical bank and Rick's throat constricted in horror.

The black plane was diving right at his Cub!

Rick shoved the nose of his plane down, wincing as the black biplane screamed by so close that the Cub was tossed around in its prop blast. It vanished behind his tail and he flew straight and level, his scalp prickling. The black plane wasn't through with him yet. He expected it to come roaring down past his nose, and he was waiting tensely, ready to fight the Cub back to level flight. If the bigger plane got too close, its prop blast would throw the Cub into a spin.

But the black plane edged slowly into sight, throttled down to Rick's own speed. He watched the blunt radial engine with its disk of propeller creep even with him. He saw the pilot, his face hidden by big goggles, motion with a gloved fist.

Rick couldn't believe his eyes. The pilot was imperiously motioning him to land! He shook his head and waved the pilot away, warning him not to come nearer.

The black plane's reply was to rock up on a wing and slide close, so close that it almost overlapped the tiny Cub. Rick slid away, sweat starting out on his face.

The strange pilot gestured again, then passed his hand across his throat. The motion said as plainly as though he had spoken: "Go down, or I'll knock you down."

Rick knew he could do it, too. The black plane could "spin him in" with hardly any danger to itself. If the pilot were desperate enough, he could take a bite out of Rick's tail with his prop.

There was only one thing to do. Rick nodded acceptance of the order, then shrugged, indicating that he didn't know where he was supposed to land. The pilot pointed ahead to a grassy stretch surrounded by woods, the only possible landing place in sight. Rick nodded again and put the Cub's nose down.

As his altimeter slowly spun around to fifteen hundred feet, then a thousand, he searched frantically for a way out. The black plane was riding slightly behind him and to the right, in position to flash across his nose at the slightest wrong move.

The strange pilot was flying at near-stalling speed, Rick knew. The biplane was a fast job, with a top speed of over two hundred miles an hour. He estimated quickly. The black plane, being heavier and faster, would take longer to turn, or longer to pull out of a dive.

Rick wiped perspiration from his forehead. He had a plan. He thought it would work, but he wasn't too sure about it.

He glued his eyes to the terrain ahead. The flat land had given way to rolling wooded country. That much was in his favor. A glance at the altimeter showed him that he had five hundred feet. The black plane was edging closer, the pilot motioning toward the clearing ahead.

Rick suddenly put the Cub's nose down. Trees flashed up to meet him. He held the dive as long as he dared, then pulled out, praying that the wings would stay on. The small plane wasn't stressed for diving. When he leveled off, his wheels were almost brushing the treetops. He turned his head and caught a glimpse of the black plane vanishing behind his tail. Then he looked straight ahead and concentrated grimly on escaping.

Unless the strange pilot were completely insane, he would never try to dive on the Cub when it was flying at treetop height. The bigger plane would not be able to pull out in time.

Rick kept as close to the ground as the trees allowed, taking advantage of every dip in the terrain. At one time he saw the black plane flash overhead and he had to fight to keep the Cub's wings level as turbulent air rocked them. But as the miles flowed underneath, he began to breathe easier. As long as he stayed near the ground, he was reasonably safe. Evidently the strange pilot valued his neck too much to try tricks without sufficient altitude.

Rick had read of war pilots "hedgehopping" to bomb an enemy, or to strafe, but he didn't know that he had effectively copied a device used by light-plane pilots to escape from fast enemy fighters.

Spindrift Island loomed across the treetops, the most welcome sight Rick had ever seen. The black plane flew past, a good fifty feet higher than he, and the pilot shook his fist, then banked away.

Rick gave a deep, grateful sigh. The stranger had given up the chase; he was safe.

In a few moments the Cub was secure on the grass strip at the edge of the island. Rick sat perfectly still for a full minute, trying to gain control of his unsteady nerves. Finally he reached with shaking hand for the package he had obtained at Cotter's and climbed out. As he did so, he looked up. The sky was empty.

"Now what did he want with me?" he asked himself. "He was trying to force me down for something." He looked at the package in his hand. "Not for this. They could get one at any electronics store." He shook his head hopelessly and turned toward the house.

As he reached the gravel path, he saw Scotty.

"What's up?" Rick called.

"Everything's quiet," Scotty answered, reaching his side. "How did you do?"

"Not so quiet," Rick said grimly. "Our playmates came up in the sky after me this time!"

Scotty's mouth fell open. As they headed toward the laboratory Rick gave him a swift summary of what had happened.

"Listen, this is getting serious," Scotty said. "We'd better do something, get some help!"

They stopped in front of the laboratory and Rick's

voice fell to a whisper. "Help? From whom? We don't know whom we can trust here, and my father won't be back for a couple of days."

"How about the police?"

Rick looked at him sidewise. "Do you think they'd take us seriously after that shields thing? Nope. We're on our own, Scotty."

He walked into the laboratory, saw Zircon and Stringfellow at work, and handed the package to the thin scientist.

"What I can't figure out is why they wanted to force me down," he said when he rejoined Scotty.

"It beats me," Scotty agreed. "Unless you had something in the plane that they wanted."

"But what? Not that coil. They could get one anywhere."

They walked in silence for a few steps. Then Rick suggested, "Let's go down to the plane."

"I should think you'd have had your fill of that thing for today," Scotty said.

"I want to look at that tail-assembly inspection port," Rick remarked.

As they reached the Cub's side, Rick walked directly to the little door in the tail and opened it. He slammed it hard to see if it would bounce open, but it stayed fast.

"Nothing loose about that thing," Scotty commented.

Rick scratched his head. "Funny," he said. "There'd be no reason for anyone to open that purposely."

Scotty examined the door. "What's it for?"

Rick started back toward the house. "It's there so you can inspect the cables in the tail assembly."

"I thought that's where you carried your lunch," Scotty joked.

"By golly, it would be big enough to carry a lunch in at that," Rick exclaimed. "Or something else!"

Scotty's head snapped back toward the little door. "Something else!" he blurted. "What a pair of dopes we are. That's it!" He dived toward the tail but Rick was there before him.

"Maybe," Rick said, crossing his fingers. "Let's see." He pried the little door open and reached inside.

"I've got something!" he shouted.

In the next second he drew out a folded slip of paper.

"What is it?" Scotty exclaimed, leaping to his side.

Rick unfolded the paper with shaking fingers. " 'Two . . . six . . . eleven . . . nine,' " he read slowly. "The rest of the sheet looks just like it. A bunch of numbers."

The boys stared at each other and then Rick let out a whoop. "It's a message! The traitor has been using my plane to send code messages to his confederates on the mainland."

CHAPTER X

A Message in Code

"Boy, what nerve this gang has," Scotty marveled. "Using you to help wreck your dad's experiment."

"But how did they do it? Who picked up the messages on the mainland?"

The two boys stared at each other for a moment and the same thought leaped into their minds.

"Mac! That new attendant!"

"Yes," Scotty said. "Didn't Gus say he thought Mac was responsible for that door being open?"

"He must be the one."

"What'll we do—decode this note, or call Gus and tell him to grab that Mac character?"

Rick looked at the coded note in his hand. "It's Greek to me and it'll take some time to make sense out of it. Let's call Gus."

They turned from the plane and ran full speed back to the house. In less than thirty seconds Rick heard the operator ringing the Whiteside Airport number.

"Gus here, who's there?" he finally heard the mechanic say.

"Gus? This is Rick. Listen, where's your new mechanic?"

"He'll be in jail, if I can get my hands on him!" Gus bellowed. "You know what he did? A California plane came in right after you left—a black biplane. I told Gus to service it while the pilot went into town for some chow—"

"And Mac stole the plane," Rick said grimly. "Is that it?"

"How did you know?"

"He chased me and tried to force me down."

Gus made harsh noises into the phone. "That's one more thing, then. So help me, if I get that guy I'll hang him with my own hands!"

"Did he bring the plane back?"

"Yeah. He landed and left it at the end of the runway and beat it into the woods. Did he hurt you, Rick?"

"He tried hard enough," Rick said. "Listen, Gus, report him to the Civil Air people. My dad will file charges when he comes back."

"Right," Gus promised. "But I don't get it. What did he want to force you down for?"

"We'll ask him when we find him," Rick said, and rang off.

He turned to Scotty. "Well, that solves that mystery."

Scotty nodded. "He didn't get the message out of the

Cub, so he got panicky and stole that visiting plane."

"His boss must be a tough customer for him to want to take a chance like that."

"Boy, that was a clever trick," Scotty said. "Planting a guy at the airport to pick up those notes every time you flew in. That's how the traitor notified the gang to buy up all those tubes. And when you had to drive to Newark, they got their chance to do it."

"Sure," Rick answered. "And I'll bet Mac was responsible for that blowout that delayed me, too. It would only have taken him a second to make a cut in the tire. I'll have to ask Gus to look at it, to make sure."

"Well, no use crying over it," Scotty remarked. "If we can decode this note, we may get him and the rest of the gang with him."

Rick looked closely at the number-covered sheet. "I don't know beans about codes," he said. "How can we decipher this thing?"

"Your father has a large library. Would he have a book on cryptography?"

"On what?" Rick asked.

"Just one of my thousand-dollar words," Scotty said, grinning. "Means the study of codes."

"Say," Rick nodded. "I do seem to remember a book like that. Come on." He started for the library with Scotty close behind. They found a heavy book titled *Cryptography for the Student.* For a half hour the two boys studied it, trying to find a code like the one on the paper Rick had found in his plane.

"No soap," he said finally. "There isn't a code anything like this in here."

"Wait a minute!" Scotty exclaimed. "It seems to me when I was in the service I heard of a code—" He stopped.

"Come on, come on!" Rick said. "Like this one, you mean?"

Scotty nodded thoughtfully. "Let me see. It was based on a book."

"I don't get it," Rick said.

"Well," Scotty began uncertainly. "With this code you choose a book—like the dictionary or something. Then all your messages are written in numbers. The first number corresponds to the page, the second one to the position of the word on the page. Unless you know the book, you can't break the code."

Rick was not discouraged. "Whoever sent this message from the island here must have a copy of the book this code is based on. Why not look around?"

Scotty nodded and closed the book. The boys headed for the scientists' quarters. No one seemed to be around. They decided to look in Zircon's office first.

Rick had a strong feeling of guilt as he started searching. Scotty stood guard at the door, in case anyone happened along.

Books, hundreds of them, stared back from the shelves and the desks. It seemed useless even to begin a search, but he looked quickly through random volumes, hoping to discover something. As the last book was leafed through, he looked at Scotty, completely discouraged.

"There's nothing here. Or maybe there is. I can't tell." He indicated the stacks of books. "It could be any one of them. All we can do is hope there's something odd about the right one. Let's take a look in Weiss's office."

In the little scientist's room the prospects were even less encouraging.

"Why do scientists read so much?" Rick complained. "There must be a hundred books in this one case."

"And all in sets, too," Scotty remarked, reaching for a book.

Rick began examining the titles. "Here's a set of ten volumes on chemical reactions, and here's another on thermodynamics. All sets."

"Hey, wait a minute," Scotty said suddenly. "Look at this." He held a thick, red-bound volume in his hands.

"What is it?"

"*Psychiatry Simplified*. It's the only book that's not part of a set. I wonder . . ."

Rick took the coded note from his pocket and spread it on the desk. "We'll soon see. The first number in a series tells the page?"

"That's right."

"The page is number two, then." He turned to the second page. "The next number is six. That means the sixth word, right?"

Scotty nodded. "And look what the word is."

"It's 'dear,'" Rick said excitedly. "The first word in a letter!"

"Go on—go on," Scotty urged, his voice shaking.

Rick's eyes flashed from code to book and his hands wrote the words that the code provided. Slowly a look of confusion spread over his face, and when the last word of the letter had been decoded, he dropped his pencil and stared at the translation.

"It—it's a love letter," he gasped.

Scotty snatched the deciphered note from his hand. "Well, I'm a ring-tailed coot," he said. "We've run into a double code!"

"You mean the code book led into another code?"

"Sure," Scotty answered. "This love letter is coded too."

"Then maybe we can decipher this one from the cryptography book," Rick said. "Come on."

The two boys went back to Hartson Brant's library. Again they took the heavy cryptography volume from the shelf, and for a long while they searched its pages.

"Nope," Scotty said finally. "This code isn't in the book either."

"Boy, this gang is really taking no chances," Rick remarked.

"But don't forget where the code led us," Scotty reminded him.

"To Weiss's office—yes. I'd say we had the goods on him."

"Don't forget, Zircon looked like the traitor, too," Scotty cautioned.

"It's really a mess," Rick declared. "But this is something concrete. I think we'd better see Weiss right now."

"Roger," Scotty said. "Get that coded note. Maybe it's in his handwriting. That would really be proof."

Sudden realization flashed into Rick's eyes. "Holy smokes! I left it back on the desk in his office!"

They scrambled for the door and ran across the big yard. Rick looked frantically around on the desk where he had spread the code note.

It was gone!

"Well, if I don't take the fur-lined dunce cap," he moaned. "Our only scrap of real evidence and I handed it right back to the traitor!"

"I think even without the note we've got the goods on Weiss," Scotty declared. "And I think we should go find him."

They walked down the office-lined hall. As they came to Zircon's door they looked in and saw him sitting at his desk, reading.

"Have you seen Professor Weiss, sir?" Rick asked.

The huge scientist looked up impatiently. "I don't keep track of the personnel here," he grumbled.

Rick turned away, taken aback by the man's gruff manner, and as he did so he stared straight into Scotty's amazed eyes.

"Look!" Scotty whispered hoarsely. "That book he's reading."

Rick spun around and stared at the volume in Hobart Zircon's big fist. It was a copy of *Psychiatry Simplified*.

"The code volume," Rick gasped. "But I just saw it in Weiss's office."

"Don't you get it?" Scotty asked. "He has a copy, too. For all we know, every scientist on the island may have one."

"No, it can't be," Rick said uncertainly. "We couldn't run into this kind of luck."

"We'd better investigate," Scotty suggested. "Come on back to your father's library."

They ran from the building and back into the big house. Even before he walked to the main shelf, Rick's eyes caught a flash of red binding. It was another copy of *Psychiatry Simplified*.

Rick sank into a leather chair and dropped his head into his hands. "What luck! Any man on the island could have sent that note. Even my father! But why do you suppose they all have a copy?"

"Well, at least we know how the traitor has been

getting his messages off the island," Scotty consoled. "And they won't be able to use it again."

"But how does this gang get in touch with the traitor?" Rick asked.

"Couldn't they phone?"

"They wouldn't dare, knowing Barby is the operator and loves to listen in on every conversation."

"Then they'd have to smuggle messages in, just as they smuggled them off. In your plane, maybe."

Rick shook his head. "No, they wouldn't take chances like that. It has to be some other way. Wigwag, maybe. Or flashers. But they'd be too easily detected. Maybe signs."

Both boys froze at the word "sign."

"The barn!" Rick gasped. "The sign on the barn. Remember how it was changed so oddly?"

"You're right," Scotty exulted. "And I'll bet we could read one of their messages if we had some binoculars!"

"Weiss's binoculars!" Rick exclaimed, rising. "Let's go."

As they entered the little scientist's office, Rick's eyes went to the bookstand where he had seen the glasses the day before.

"Not here," Scotty said.

"I'd say those binoculars are with Weiss," Rick said. "And I'd say Weiss would be at the tidal flats. Let's go find him."

The path to the tidal flats seemed torturingly long, despite their rapid strides. Then, as they turned off the last twist of the path, Rick jerked to a stop. He pointed silently.

There, on the edge of the cliff, sat a man with his eyes glued to a pair of binoculars pointed straight at the barn, across on the mainland. But it was not Weiss. It was John Stringfellow!

CHAPTER XI

The Adventure in the Old Barn

"And look what he has there beside him," Scotty whispered.

Rick saw the leaves of a book fluttering in the breeze, and red binding flashing in the sun. It was a copy of *Psychiatry Simplified*.

He attempted to move back into the shadow of the trees, but just as he did, his foot slipped and he scattered pebbles over the face of the rock.

John Stringfellow's head jerked almost imperceptibly, but in a split second he had returned his gaze to the barn across the water.

"Did he see us?" Rick whispered.

"I don't know," Scotty answered, "but I don't see any sense in pussyfooting. Let's go talk to him."

They walked out from the shadow of the trees and headed boldly for Stringfellow.

He turned just as they arrived at his side, and smiled up at them. "Out for a stroll, boys?"

"Yes," Rick replied. "What are you doing to amuse yourself, sir?"

The thin scientist looked out toward the sea and placed the binoculars to his eyes. "I'm making a survey of the bird species around the island," he said calmly. "Very wide variety in this area."

"May I take a look?" Rick asked, extending his hand for the binoculars.

The glasses dropped slowly from Stringfellow's eyes. "I'm afraid Professor Weiss is pretty particular about who handles his glasses," he said.

"Oh, one look wouldn't hurt," Rick insisted.

He was certain now that Stringfellow didn't want strange eyes looking at the barn across the way. But to his surprise the scientist said, "Well, I suppose one look wouldn't hurt." He held the glasses out to Rick.

Scotty watched tensely as Rick fastened the binoculars to his eyes and twisted the adjustment screw. For a full thirty seconds the boy held the glasses on the barn sign. Finally he handed them back to the scientist.

"Thank you," he said. "Well, shall we walk awhile longer, Scotty?"

Scotty could hardly wait until they reached the path, out of Stringfellow's hearing.

"What about it?" he whispered.

"No message," Rick said flatly.

"But the book on his lap," Scotty protested. "That's the finger of guilt if I ever saw one!"

"I agree with you," Rick answered. "But the finger of guilt has pointed to everyone on the island so far. This gives us just one more suspect."

"But what are we going to do?" Scotty asked as they turned up the path. "Are we going to just sit and wait for the traitor's next move?"

"Make a suggestion," Rick said wryly. "I've run out of ideas."

Scotty thought for a minute. "How about the love letter? We should make some attempt to get it decoded," he suggested.

"That's right," Rick said. "Maybe Jerry Webster knows some code expert. He gets around a lot and knows some important people. I'll call him and ask."

He reached for the phone and soon was connected with the *Morning Record*. Jerry Webster answered, and Rick swiftly outlined his problem to the young reporter.

"Yes, a friend of mine, Hume Wallace, is a cryptographer," Jerry told him. "But it may take a couple of days for him to work it out."

Rick read the love letter to him and urged him to get it decoded as soon as possible. As he hung up, he said to Scotty, "That's our biggest lead to the traitor. If we get that letter decoded, there may be a signature on it."

"You hope!" Scotty said.

"Yes, and I still say that sign on the barn figures in the traitor's plans. I say we should go take a close look at it."

"Okay," Scotty answered. "Let's go."

As they left the house, Dismal ran to greet them, barking excitedly. Rick, busy speculating about the meaning of the changing sign, greeted him without the usual enthusiasm. The pup, hurt feelings showing in the dejected slump of his tail, fell in step.

A flight of wooden stairs led down to the cove in which the island boats were tied up. Rick chose the fast fifteen-footer and motioned to Scotty to get in.

Dismal barked excitedly, his sad eyes pleading. "Not today, boy," Rick said.

The pup barked again, then rolled over and played dead.

Rick couldn't resist. "Oh, all right. Come on," he said.

Dismal leaped into the rear seat, panting his excitement as the engine roared into life.

Rick reversed the engine, backed out, then he swung the boat around and gave it throttle. The stern bit into the swells and the bow lifted, pointing toward the mainland. Spray whipped against the windshield as the boat took the swells.

Rick held the boat steady on a course that would

bring them to the point nearest the barn. While he let the craft drift into the wooded bank, Scotty leaped out of the cockpit and pulled them up to a convenient tree with the boat hook; then he tied the boat fast.

"About half a mile to go," Rick said. They trudged through the woods and into the plowed fields, Dismal ranging far ahead, his nose busy with new scents.

"What do you expect to find?" Scotty asked.

"I don't know," Rick confessed. "Maybe nothing. But I won't be satisfied until I've had a look."

They could see the sign clearly now; then the barn itself. It looked deserted, but they waited at the edge of the field for long minutes.

"Nothing there," Scotty said. "Not even a cow."

Rick leaped lightly over the wire fence and led the way to the barn. At the door they stopped again, looking around to be sure they were alone. "It's all right, I guess," he said, and they went in.

It was dim inside the barn. Rick looked around, searching for he didn't know what. He could see at once that the barn was empty. He guessed by the few remnants of moldy hay in the mow that it hadn't been used for years.

"Nothing here," Scotty commented.

"Except mice." Rick pointed to Dismal, who was scrambling across the floor after a tiny mouse. The pup ran head-on into the wall—and it gave out a hollow sound.

"Hey! Did you hear that?" Rick exclaimed.

In an instant he was investigating. His probing fingers found a loose board. He tugged, and it came away, revealing a hidden closet.

Scotty bent and peered into the hole. Getting up, he said in disgust, "Paint! Nothing but a few old cans of paint and some brushes."

"Let's see." Rick sniffed. "Turpentine. These brushes have been used, and not so very long ago."

"What does that mean?"

"Well, the sign has been changed, hasn't it? Whoever did it used this paint."

"And what does that tell us?"

"Nothing." Rick slammed the board back into place, a little more violently than necessary. "Exactly nothing!"

He winced as Scotty's fingers dug into his arm. "Hey, what—?"

Then he saw what had startled the other boy. Dismal was crouched at the entrance, growling. At that moment, Rick heard the approaching drone of a car engine.

"Someone's coming," he gasped. He called Dismal to his side. "Stay with me, boy. We don't want them to see you." He joined Scotty in looking for an observation post.

Knotholes provided ports through which they could see across the field nearest the road. Rick put his eye to one, moving his head back and forth as he searched for the car.

"Scotty, I see it," he said hoarsely. "It's the same gray sedan!"

"We've got to get out of here, Rick."

"But how can we? If we start across the field, they'll see us."

Scotty's alert eyes were busy. Suddenly he pointed upward. "The hayloft. We can hide up there."

Rick didn't stop to comment. He ran for the ladder that led to the loft. At the bottom he stopped short. "Diz! Here, boy!" He scooped up the dog and made his way up the ladder as rapidly as he could with one hand. Scotty was right behind him.

The loft was dusty, and rays of sunlight came in through cracks in the roof, but the floor boards were still fairly tightly joined. No one could see them from below.

Rick lay flat, moving back and forth until he found a crack in the wall. He looked out at the gray car, parked now, its doors open.

His heart climbed into his throat and stuck there. Four men were getting out—the two men who looked like prize fighters, the bearded man, and a man with a hideously scarred face whom he had never seen before.

"Scotty," Rick whispered.

Scotty had found a crack of his own. "I see them," he whispered hoarsely.

The men walked toward the barn and vanished from

sight. In a moment Rick heard them enter the big room below. He crouched silently, hardly daring to breathe.

"Kogan," an authoritative voice commanded, "get the paint."

That must be the man with the scarred face, Rick thought. He knew it wasn't the voice of any of the others.

There was a rattle as the board was pulled away from the cupboard, and then a coarse voice said, "Looks like someone's been at this stuff."

"Are you certain?"

That was the bearded man. Rick froze.

"Looks like it, Carlos. The board was partly open. I shut it tight when we left."

"Probably a chance prowler," Scarface said. "No matter. He could learn nothing from a little paint."

From beside Rick came a low, rising rumble. He reached out desperately. Dismal was now convinced that something was wrong. He was going to bark!

Rick clamped his hands over the dog's muzzle just as the bark rose in his throat. Diz sniffed, and the rumble died.

Rick wiped sweat from his face. Close!

"Let's get this job over and get back to the plant," Scarface said. "Get the ladder and climb up, Kogan. Paste 'Smoke' over 'Drink' and I'll read you the numbers."

So that was it! "Smoke" was changed to "Drink" and back again by just pasting the word on!

Dismal was suffering again. "Quiet, pup!" Rick whispered desperately.

It had been a mistake to clamp down on the pup's nose. Now his nose was tickling and he wanted to sneeze. Rick stroked the dog's head, trying to soothe the sneeze away.

Scotty slid across the floor. "What's up?" he asked almost inaudibly.

Rick fought down a hysterical desire to laugh. "He has to sneeze."

Scotty patted the pup's head. "Sh-h-h, boy." His eyes were anguished as they met Rick's.

Dismal sniffed a couple of times.

There was the scraping of a ladder, and then the light through the wide cracks in the roof was suddenly blotted out.

Rick grabbed Scotty's arm. Kogan was right over their heads! He pointed up and Scotty nodded. Through the cracks they could see the dark blot of Kogan's body. He was evidently the thug in the sports coat.

Below, Scarface was reading monotonously, " 'Twenty-four, seventeen, nineteen, thirty-six, twelve . . .' "

It was the code! Kogan was painting it on the sign, right over their heads!

Dismal sniffed.

Kogan's foot scraped as he worked on the sign.

Rick and Scotty sat frozen.

Dismal sniffed again.

Then, so suddenly that Rick jumped, Scotty whipped off his jacket and covered Dismal with it. From under the jacket came a sneeze that sounded like a thunderclap!

"Hey, did you scrape that ladder?" Kogan demanded.

The boys weren't even breathing. Their eyes were on the bulk that blocked the light above them.

"Paint the numbers," Scarface said. "Don't worry about the ladder."

"I heard something," Kogan insisted.

" 'Forty-five,' " Scarface droned.

Rick relaxed. Scarface was going to ignore Kogan's sharp ears. They heard the paintbrush scrape against the roof just above them as the man added the number to the sign.

"That's the last one," Scarface told him. "Come down."

They heard steps on the ladder and then a thump as the man's feet hit the ground. "Listen, I know I heard something," Kogan said.

Rick stiffened again.

Scarface spoke in cold, flat tones. "Kogan, I can't afford to have men working for me who have jumpy nerves. We heard nothing."

"Okay," Kogan growled.

The boys heard the boards rattle as the paint cans were replaced. Rick applied his eye to the crack in the wall again and saw the men walk toward the gray sedan. The motor roared to life and in a moment the car was speeding across the field toward the highway.

Dismal put back his head and sneezed.

Rick and Scotty began to laugh, weak with relief. "Sneeze again," Rick said. "Bark your head off. They're gone."

Dismal lay down and rolled over.

"You should have played dead a few minutes ago," Scotty said. "Come on, dog, let's go." He picked up the pup and carried him down the ladder.

After a cautious look around, to be sure no member of the gang had been left behind, the boys dashed outside for a look at the sign.

SMOKE WHITE CREAM, it proclaimed.

But of the numbers which they had heard Scarface read off, there was absolutely no trace!

"Well, I'll be doggoned." Rick looked at the sign and then at Scotty.

"Where are they?" Scotty asked.

"We heard Scarface reading off the numbers, and we heard that Kogan guy painting them on. They have to be here!"

"But they're not," Scotty protested.

Rick turned back into the barn. "I want a look at that paint," he said.

He selected a can with wet paint on its top and pulled it out. It was ordinary white paint, the same as used in the background color on the sign.

"Just ordinary white paint, as far as I can see," he said. He held the can out toward Scotty. The marine bent to look at the mixture, and just at that moment Dismal decided that he was being ignored. With a little whine, he rolled over on his back at Scotty's knee, and his legs were flung into the air, straight against the side of the can. The can slipped from Rick's grasp, and white paint cascaded over the dog's fur.

"Diz, you dope!" Rick moaned.

With handkerchiefs and scraps of hay, they cleaned the dog's fur as best they could; then they picked him up bodily and carried him back to the boat.

As they roared off toward the island, Rick looked back at the sign and shook his head.

"Scotty," he said, "I can't help feeling that the key to the whole business is right in our hands. And we're just too dumb to see it."

CHAPTER XII

Dismal Does His Bit

IT HAD been the busiest and certainly the most adventurous day in Rick's life. But, tired as he was, sleep came reluctantly.

After half an hour of tossing restlessly, he looked in on Scotty. That young man was sprawled flat, dead to the world. Rick looked at him enviously and went back to his own room.

He picked up the spark coil and tinkered with it for a while, making the connections. He attached the small flashlight batteries and pushed the button. The coil buzzed very satisfactorily. The wire was connected to the output of the coil. Now, if he held the wire in his hand and pressed the button, anything he might touch would get a dose of electric current.

He put the gadget down listlessly. It had seemed like a good idea when he had started working on it. Now, in the light of recent happenings on Spindrift, it seemed like a waste of time. He got back in bed and tried to will himself to sleep.

He blinked sleepily and his eyes closed. His hand fumbled for the bed switch that turned out the lights. The room faded and gave way to the shadowy land between full sleep and awakening. He tossed a little, and finally drifted into sleep.

Then suddenly he was standing up, poised to jump, his eyes wide open. A horrible scream was still ringing in his ears.

"Barby!" He threw open his door and ran down the hall, Scotty right behind him. Other doors were opening as the household jerked to startled wakefulness.

They found Barby standing on her bed, one hand across her eyes, the other with a firm grip on the bedpost. At her feet crouched a very unhappy Dismal.

"Take him away! Please, someone take him away!" she cried.

Rick lifted her down bodily. "Barby, what is it? Were you dreaming?"

She lifted a tear-streaked face. "Rick, Dismal's dead. He's a ghost, I saw him!"

Scotty was speechless.

Rick hushed her frightened cries. "It's all right, sis. Diz is okay. Look at him. He's worried about you."

The pup was looking up and his tail thumped hopefully. There was anguish in his sad eyes. He knew he had caused all the rumpus, but he didn't know why.

Neither did Rick. "Look at him, Barby," he pleaded. "He's all right."

Scotty picked Dismal up and held him close. At the feel of his cold tongue on her cheek, Barby gave a little jump; then she reached out a frightened hand and stroked his head.

"Diz," she said. "You're all right, Diz?"

"Sure he is," Scotty assured her.

Rick led her to a chair. "Sit down, sis. Now tell us what happened."

Barby closed her eyes and shuddered. "Rick, I was so frightened! I got into bed and turned out the light, and when I looked over in the corner, there was Diz. He— he was all bright and spooky—like a ghost. I screamed, I guess." She gave them an apologetic little smile.

"I should think you would," Scotty said.

The rest of the household was crowding into the room now.

"You must have been dreaming, dear," Mrs. Brant said.

"No," Barby insisted. "I hadn't gone to sleep yet."

"Of course you had," Hobart Zircon insisted. "It's a common thing not to know one has fallen asleep."

Rick counted noses swiftly. Weiss and Stringfellow were missing. He asked Zircon where they were.

"Guarding the lab and the launcher," the huge man said. "Against what, I don't know."

Rick whispered to his mother, "Get them out, Mom. I want to talk with Barby alone."

She shooed the others back to their rooms, assuring them that Barby was all right. Then she turned to Rick. "What is it, dear? Don't you think Barby was dreaming?"

"No," Rick said. "I don't, Mom."

He sat down beside his sister. "What were you doing, just before you went to bed?"

Barby hesitated and then said, "I was getting a tan."

"A tan?" Scotty looked incredulous.

"With Rick's ultraviolet lamp," she confessed. She indicated the lamp in the corner. "It's July already, and I haven't any tan at all and I wanted to catch up with the rest of the girls."

"What about Diz, though?" Rick interrupted.

"He took a sun bath with me." She giggled a little at the thought.

Rick was thoughtfully silent for a moment.

"So that's it," he announced. "Diz got into some paint today, and that paint must have been sensitive to ultraviolet light. It glowed, that's all." He rose and walked to the ultraviolet lamp and switched it on. Then he turned off the overhead light.

Dismal walked into the light to sniff. Rick waited a second and then snapped the ultraviolet lamp off. Dismal glowed a ghostly blue.

"Well, that answers the mystery of Dismal then," Barby said as Rick turned the lights back on.

"That isn't the only mystery it solves," Rick remarked, looking at Scotty as he spoke. "Think you can sleep now, Barby?"

"Yes. And I'm sorry about the screams."

Mrs. Brant kissed her daughter good night, and Rick and Scotty walked from the room with Dismal at their heels.

"Well, now we know why we couldn't see the numbers on that sign," Rick said after he closed the door behind them. "Those numbers would only be visible through special lenses that could pick up ultraviolet light."

"But there's ultraviolet in the sunlight," Scotty said. "How come that didn't make it glow so we could see them?"

"There's not a high enough concentration of ultraviolet in sunlight," Rick explained. "Special lenses would have to be turned on the paint to see it."

"That white paint was the thing then, huh?"

Rick nodded.

"And the numbers weren't painted there until after we saw Stringfellow looking at the barn. That's why we couldn't see them through his binoculars."

"Either that, or those glasses weren't equipped with special lenses at all."

"Which would make him innocent," Scotty offered.

"Not necessarily," Rick said. "He might have been

looking to see if there was a message. Besides, he had the code book with him. And he was looking at that sign on the barn."

"He sounds guilty all right."

"I'm sure he's guilty," Rick said.

Scotty grinned sourly. "Seems to me I've heard that song before," he said. "About Weiss and Zircon."

Rick groaned. "I know it, I know it! We were just as positive before and just as wrong. Let's admit it. We still haven't found our traitor."

Dismal wandered in, sidling up to the boys sheepishly.

"Here's the ghost." Scotty grinned.

Rick bent down to scratch the pup's ribs. Diz promptly rolled over, all four legs in the air.

"Sometimes I think you're not very bright," Rick told him, laughing. "But spilling that paint was the smartest bit of detecting any of us have done so far."

Dismal groaned his satisfaction, his hind legs flailing the air as Rick scratched his ribs.

"Maybe we'd better turn over the whole business to Diz," Scotty said. "He's come closer to solving it than we have."

CHAPTER XIII

The Missing Microtron

RICK awoke from deep, exhausted sleep with Scotty shaking him.

"Hit the deck," Scotty teased. "You going to sleep all day?"

"Go away," Rick mumbled. Then he turned over and buried his face in the pillow.

"It's half-past ten," Scotty pleaded. "Roll out and come on down to breakfast. I'm starved."

Rick sat up and rubbed sleep from his eyes. "All right," he answered grumpily.

"I'll be downstairs, sleep fiend," Scotty said.

Rick swung out of bed reluctantly. He felt as though another ten hours of sleep would just suit him. But Scotty was right, he couldn't sleep all day.

He quickly washed and dressed. Hurrying downstairs, he was amazed at the vitality that grew in him at the smell of bacon and eggs.

114

Stringfellow and Weiss were seated at the table, already hard at work on their late breakfast. Rick greeted them, though a little coolly. He had the uncomfortable feeling that with each "good morning" he might be addressing a traitor.

"We've been up all night," Stringfellow explained. "I stayed at the launcher and Julius guarded the laboratory. Tonight Scotty and Zircon will act as guards."

"Fine," Scotty said. "Where is Mr. Zircon now?"

"At the lab," Stringfellow answered.

Rick sat down to breakfast, concentrating on his bacon and eggs. He didn't feel like engaging in conversation with the two scientists.

"How can I be cordial to any of them?" he thought. "They've *all* been acting suspiciously. How do I know which one is selling us out?"

Dismal nuzzled his leg and Rick fed him a small scrap of bacon. The pup put it down on the floor and stared at it for a few moments before eating it.

"It's all right. It's safe. Go on and eat it, dopey."

Dismal downed it in one gulp and waited expectantly for more.

"Rick!" Mrs. Brant frowned from the doorway. "Are you feeding Dismal at the table again?"

He said, "I'm sorry, Mom."

She called to the pup, and he followed her into the kitchen. Rick smiled to himself. His mother was very strict about feeding Diz at the table; but she was the first to put aside small scraps for him.

At that moment Hobart Zircon barged into the dining room like a huge whirlwind. His face was red with anger and his voice boomed out at everyone there.

"Which one of you took the microtron tube?"

There was an instant of stunned silence; then they all were talking at once.

Julius Weiss demanded shrilly, "Are you accusing us of stealing the microtron, Hobart?"

Rick jumped to his feet. "Are you sure it's gone, Professor?"

"Sure? Of course I'm sure! The socket is empty!"

It was Stringfellow who restored order. "Listen, everyone. Please, gentlemen. One at a time. You're certain it is not in the lab, Hobart?"

"Didn't I say so? I looked everywhere!"

Stringfellow's calm eyes went from one to another. "This is serious. But somehow, I just can't believe the tube is missing. Rick, it seems to me your father mentioned something about taking it with him. Did he say anything to you?"

"No, sir," Rick said definitely. "Why would he take the tube with him to New York?"

"I haven't the faintest idea," Stringfellow said. "Your father is in charge. I certainly wouldn't question his actions."

"If that is true," Zircon bellowed, "then we have no need to worry. But if Hartson does not have the tube—"

"But he must have," Weiss interjected. "Surely no one would steal it. Of what use would it be to anyone but us?"

"What is this tube, anyway?" Scotty asked.

"A special one that was made right here in the lab," Rick explained. "It's the only one of its kind. And it's the most important part of the rocket control."

"Exactly," Stringfellow said. "It was made for this special purpose. No one would have anything to gain by stealing it."

Rick could have said something at this point, but he kept silent.

"We will search the laboratory," Stringfellow decided. "If the tube is not found, we must conclude that Hartson has it."

As the scientists hurried to the lab, Scotty asked, "You're sure your father wouldn't take it?"

"Why on earth would Dad take it?"

"For safekeeping. Or maybe to have a duplicate one made—just in case."

"Possible, but not probable," Rick said. "I'm going to call Dad."

Using the phone in Mr. Brant's office, he asked Barby to get the Whiteside operator and then placed a call to the Claymore Hotel in New York.

Scotty paced the floor, while Rick waited impatiently.

The phone buzzed. "Mr. Brant is out. He is not expected back until midafternoon. Do you wish me to call again?"

"Please," Rick replied. He hung up and turned to Scotty. "Another wait," he said. "We're always waiting."

By the time an hour had passed, Rick was growing so restless he couldn't keep still. He glared at Scotty, who was absorbed in a book.

"Don't you ever get nervous?"

"Sure, but what's the sense in wearing a groove in the floor?"

"This is getting me down. I'm going out to the lab."

He went upstairs and picked up his spark-coil contrivance, intending to put the finishing touches to the gadget. Keeping his hands busy might keep his mind from turning over the same old questions again and again.

As he went out of the house, Scotty fell in step. "I'll go along and watch," he said. "The book wasn't very good."

Rick grinned. "You're as nervous as I am. You just keep it under cover better."

"Could be." Scotty admitted, grinning too.

The big, main room with its workbenches and test equipment was deserted. Rick placed the spark coil in a vise and made adjustments, while Scotty watched silently. Then he took friction tape and strapped the batteries to the wooden coil box, wiring the button to the top.

"It's finished," he said.

Scotty inspected it. "Good. Now what are you going to do with it?"

Rick shrugged. "Nothing." He took the length of wire in his hand and placed the hand on Scotty's shoulder. Then, so casually that his friend suspected nothing, he reached over and pushed the button.

Scotty leaped a foot in the air and let out a yelp. "Hey!"

"Now I'm sure it works," Rick said, chuckling.

"And how!" Scotty rubbed his shoulder. "The shock tied me up in knots for a minute. Don't do that again, pal!"

"I won't," Rick promised. He pushed the contrivance back under the bench shelf. "Come on, let's go see if Mom has anything for making sandwiches."

Later, armed with tall glasses of milk and sandwiches, they sat on the porch and watched a cargo ship pass by on its way to some northern port.

"I wonder who Scarface is?" Rick asked, thinking about what they had seen and heard at the barn. "Judging by the way he gave orders, he must be the boss."

"And I wonder what he meant when he said they had to get back to the plant," Scotty said thoughtfully.

The word hit Rick so hard that the glass of milk slipped from his grasp and shattered, unnoticed, on the floor.

"The plant!" he shouted. "That's it! That's why they stole the microtron tube. To use in a laboratory of their own!"

"Of course!" Scotty exclaimed. "Why didn't we think of that before? They've been stealing your father's ideas and using them in a lab just like this one!"

The two boys leaped to their feet.

"We've got to find that plant," Rick said.

"But where?"

"I don't know. Let me think." His mind raced over the incidents of the past few days. "There was the black plane. We could go look near the place where Mac tried to force me down!"

"And how about the gray car? Where were they heading, the day you followed it?"

"Not toward their lab. They'd be too smart for that," Rick said.

Inside the house, the phone jangled sharply. The boys raced into Hartson Brant's office.

"Yes?"

"On your call to New York, we are ready," the operator intoned.

In a moment, Hartson Brant's voice came through. "Hello, Rick. What is it, son?"

"Dad," Rick said, "the microtron tube is gone. Do you have it?"

There was hushed silence at the other end of the wire. Then Hartson Brant spoke again, and his voice sounded tired. "No, Rick. Have you looked everywhere?"

"Yes, sir."

"That finishes us then," the scientist said slowly. "We couldn't possibly make another one in time. And that means I'll have to tell the Stoneridge people to count us out."

"Please don't do that, Dad," Rick pleaded. "Scotty and I have an idea we want to follow up. Give us a chance. Will you, Dad?"

Hartson Brant thought it over for a moment. "All right, son. But don't do anything foolhardy. I'll take the next train home."

Rick hung up and turned to Scotty. "Did you hear?" Scotty nodded.

"Let's go," Rick said. "It isn't much of a chance, but we have to try it." He reached into a drawer of his father's desk and took out an old but good pair of field glasses. "They're not as good as Weiss's binoculars," he said. "But they may help us to spot that secret lab!"

CHAPTER XIV

Down in a Wheat Field

Rick climbed to a thousand feet and leveled off. "No need to go any higher. We couldn't see much."

Scotty nodded. "This is a good altitude—high enough to see plenty of the countryside." He took the binoculars from their case and held them to his eyes, turning the knobs to focus them properly.

"These are just the ticket," he said. "I can see practically every ant in New Jersey."

"Mosquitoes," Rick corrected. "New Jersey is famous for its mosquitoes, not its ants." His eyes were scanning the horizon as he spoke, searching for any sign that might lead them to the secret laboratory.

"What's that?" Scotty asked suddenly.

Rick followed his pointing finger. "Some sort of construction. Can't you see through the glasses?"

Scotty shook his head. "Not very clearly. It's round, I think, and pretty high."

"What!" Rick grabbed for the binoculars. "Let's see." He took the glasses and held them to his eyes, trying to make out what Scotty had seen.

The structure on the horizon was cylindrical, reaching into the air, above the treetops. He handed the glasses back to Scotty and rocked the little plane over in a tight bank, heading for the strange edifice.

"What do you make of it?" Scotty asked.

"I don't know for sure," Rick replied grimly. "But it could be a rocket-launching device. A round frame like that could support a rocket."

As they came closer to the structure, Rick put the Cub into a shallow dive, the nose pointing straight at the cylinder. Scotty shot him a worried glance which Rick interpreted correctly. "Don't worry. I'm not going to fly into it. I just want to get down where we can get a good look."

The cylinder was near a group of buildings, invisible until now because of concealing foliage and their neutral coat of paint. The structure itself glared red with fresh color, standing out sharply against the green of the surrounding trees.

Rick eased back on the control wheel as the ground flashed up. The Cub shot over the cylinder scarcely a hundred feet above ground, then zoomed skyward again.

Scotty and Rick looked at each other and suddenly they were laughing.

"Rocket launcher," Scotty said. "Oh, great!"

Rick shook his head. "You saw it first, remember? I guess neither of us would make good farmers, not even knowing a new silo when we see one."

"It was the top that fooled me," Scotty said. "I'd never seen a silo with the top off, at least not from the air."

They passed over the town of Whiteside. A mile beyond, Rick saw a clearing in the woods that looked vaguely familiar. But had the place where Mac tried to force him down been so close to the town?

He phrased the question aloud, and Scotty answered, "Could be. I don't imagine you were in a mood to notice distances with that plane on your tail."

"We'll take a look," Rick said. Again he put the Cub in a dive, holding it well above treetop level this time. The clearing passed underneath. "I didn't see a thing," Rick declared.

"Neither did I. Wait! What's that on the opposite side?"

Scotty was looking through the field glasses.

"I don't see anything," Rick said.

"Go back," Scotty said. "I want another look. I saw something gleam as we passed over. It looked like the sun on glass."

Rick banked around and brought the little plane back on a straight line with the center of the open field. This time Scotty knew where to look.

"I see it!" he exclaimed. "A car. Right at the edge of the woods." Then, as they passed close, he turned with an exultant yell. "It's the gray sedan!"

"Are you sure? Take another look, Scotty."

"Right. But I'm sure. I don't believe in coincidences. There can't be very many gray sedans of that make in this neck of the woods."

"But why should it be at the clearing? I don't see any buildings."

"Search me."

"Besides," Rick continued, "Mac wouldn't have tried to force me down over his own field. If I got away—which I did—it would be too easy to find him."

"Could be," Scotty conceded. "Well, we've found some trace of the gray car. Now what?"

"I don't know," Rick answered. "I wish we were sure."

They had been flying in a wide circle, five hundred feet above the woods. Now he turned back toward the field. "I'm going to take a closer look," he said. "Hang on to your hat."

"I haven't a hat," Scotty said grimly. "I'll hang on to my stomach if you're going to try anything fancy."

Rick let the Cub down until the wheels were almost touching the treetops, and headed straight for the gray car. As they sped across the clearing, Scotty let out a wild yell.

"Get out of here, quick! They're shooting at us!"

Rick jabbed the throttle and lifted the small plane's nose. As the edge of the clearing and the gray blur of the sedan passed below, he caught a glimpse of an orange flash.

The Cub was a thousand feet in the air before he leveled off. When he turned to Scotty his face was white. "They were really shooting," he said shakily. "You weren't just kidding!"

"Not me," Scotty answered. "I know muzzle flashes when I see 'em." He took a deep breath. "Boy, this is past the joking stage. I'm scared. If that's the kind of mugs we have to deal with, I'm thinking we'd better call out a platoon of marines."

"I've had enough," Rick said grimly. "I'm going to land at the Whiteside Airport, and then I'm going to have a talk with the police. They can't explain this away like they did the shields."

"That's the best thing to do," Scotty agreed.

Rick glanced down at the terrain below, trying to get his bearings. While they had talked, the Cub had been flying in a straight line due west.

His friend glanced down, too, then turned to him and said, "What's that white stuff?"

"What white stuff?"

"Underneath the plane." Scotty pointed to a stream of vapor that flowed beneath them.

The color washed out of Rick's face. He leaned forward and snapped off the switch, simultaneously pushing forward on the control wheel. The engine coughed once and died, leaving the propeller windmilling uncertainly.

"Hey!" cried Scotty. "What did you do that for?"

"That white stuff," Rick said tensely, "was gasoline. One spark from the exhaust and we'd have blown up."

The silence pressed in on them, relieved only by the faint sound of air rushing past the gliding plane. Scotty fell silent, tightening his safety belt. Rick leaned far out of his window, searching for the best place to put the Cub down.

The only level place in sight was a wheat field next to a large farm. It looked awfully small.

"Like trying to land on a handkerchief," Scotty said dryly.

Rick's voice sounded strained. "We'll make it. Relax."

"Who are you trying to convince?"

Rick's eyes never left the field. They were flying parallel to it, losing altitude rapidly. He had to gauge their descent just right, and make a 180-degree turn, which would end right at the boundary fence. Otherwise, they might not stop before the other fence was reached.

His hands on the control wheel were damp with sweat, and a stream of perspiration poured down his face. After pulling the plane around in a tight turn, he saw at once that he was going to overshoot the mark. He began fishtailing, kicking the rudder from one side to the other.

The boundary fence drifted past and they were over the field, the Cub wabbling from side to side. Then he pulled the control wheel all the way back. The tail went down and the nose was pointed skyward. They pancaked to earth with a jar and rolled forward through grain that was cockpit high, losing speed rapidly as they bumped over the rough earth.

When the plane came to a stop, Scotty let the air out of his lungs audibly. "Nice flying," he said. "But how are you going to get out of here?"

Rick looked around. The field was the size of a postage stamp.

"It's small," he said, "but I could make it if the wheat were cut."

"Not now, you couldn't," Scotty pointed out. "Not without gas in this thing."

"That's right," Rick said wryly. "Let's see about it." He climbed out, patted the earth lovingly and grinned up at Scotty. "I was afraid we were going to hit this ground a little harder."

As Scotty climbed out, Rick walked to the engine covering and began unsnapping the patent screws with his jackknife. In a moment he had it off and was probing the engine's innards.

"Take a look," he said, holding up a piece of the fuel line. "A hole right through it!"

"And here's where the bullet came in," Scotty said, pointing to a hole in the cowling.

"And here's where it hit," Rick added, indicating a bright splash of metal on the engine itself.

The boys looked at each other, then at the cabin, so close behind the spot where the bullet had struck.

"Look, Rick," Scotty said. "Having fist fights with this gang and doing nice, clean detective work is one thing, but having gun fights with them when they have all the guns—that's plain ridiculous!"

"I agree with you," Rick answered, looking across the top of the waving wheat. "But what can we do?"

"We can call the cops in on this. That's what we can do," Scotty said flatly. "And get in touch with your dad!"

"Right now I think we'd better prepare for another battle," Rick said, "with this farmer!"

Thrashing through the wheat toward them came a sunburned man with a pitchfork in his hand. His eyes swept the length of the destruction wrought by the Cub's forced landing and then stopped on the boys themselves.

"Well, you made a fine mess of my wheat," he said tartly.

"I'm sorry, sir," Rick said, as the farmer arrived at the plane. "We just had to come down."

"I saw you. I told my wife, 'Martha,' I said, 'I got that wheat insured against everything from hurricanes to snowstorms, but not airplanes—and I'll bet that's just where that thing's gonna land.' And it did."

"Believe me, we'd have preferred to stay in the air," Rick said earnestly. "But we'll pay for your wheat."

The farmer wiped his red face with a blue handkerchief and looked at his ruined wheat as though estimating the cost.

"Time enough for that later," he said. "My wife's worried to death about you young fools breakin' your necks in our field. You better come along and show her you're all right. How'd it happen?"

"Oh, just a little engine trouble," Rick answered, throwing a silencing wink at Scotty.

The farmer remained silent the rest of the way to the big house. As they stepped out of the field, the boys saw a motherly-looking woman in red gingham anxiously looking their way.

"They're all right, Mother," the man called. "Now," he said, turning to the boys, "how can you get that thing out of my field?"

"Well, first off, we'll need a phone. Do you have one?" Rick asked.

"Yup. Right in the livin' room."

"I'd better call Mother first," Rick said. He called the Spindrift Island number. In a moment his mother's cheerful voice answered and he explained rapidly what had happened, omitting the fact that the broken fuel line had been cut by a bullet.

"How long will it be before you can get home?" she asked.

Rick squinted out at the fast-fading light. "If I can get Gus to bring me a fuel line, I'll be home tonight, Mom. Otherwise I might have to stay here till morning."

"Well, do the best you can," his mother said. "And be careful."

Rick smiled at the slightly tardy advice, reassured her, and said good-by.

"I hope Gus can get that fuel line to us," Scotty said. "Better not waste any time calling him."

Rick called the Whiteside Airport number.

"Gus on this end. Who's on that end?"

"Rick. Gus, I'm down in a wheat field ten miles away. Do you have a fuel line in stock?"

"Sure, what's the matter?"

"Broken line," Rick said briefly. "And I'll need gas. I lost quite a bit. Can you fly it over?"

"Afraid not," Gus returned. "My kite is down for its hundred-hour check. It won't be in flying shape for a couple of days. I'll drive the stuff over."

"Okay," Rick agreed reluctantly. He gave the mechanic directions for reaching the farm, and hung up.

Scotty noticed that Rick's hands were shaking. "What's the matter?" he asked anxiously.

"I guess I'm just beginning to realize what a close

shave we had," Rick said . "Why on earth did they shoot at us do you suppose?"

"I don't know," Scotty answered. "This is the first time they've come right out and played rough—with guns. I think one of those guys lost his head."

"Well, it looks like we'll have to stay here all night," Rick said finally.

"We? Do you think it's wise?" Scotty asked.

"What do you mean?"

"Personally, I think one of us should be back on that island," Scotty said.

"You're right," Rick answered. "But I have to stay and fly the Cub out."

"I'll go back then," Scotty said. "If they've started shooting at us, who knows what they might do on that island while we're away."

When they returned to the porch, the farmer was waiting for them. "Did you get help?" he inquired.

"Yes, sir," Rick answered. "I'm afraid we'll have to stay in your wheat field overnight. I'm not equipped for night flying and my fuel line won't get here until after dark."

He turned to Scotty. "How are you going to get to Whiteside?" Rick asked.

Scotty held up his thumb. "Remember what I was using that for when you met me?" he answered, grinning. "Well, I'm going to put it to work on the road right now.

I'll ask Barby to pick me up in the speedboat when I get there."

Rick shook his head. "Be careful," he warned. "These guys are getting rough. So keep your eyes open when you get back to the island."

Scotty nodded. "Don't worry," he said. He headed out the driveway and Rick saw him disappear up the road.

The farmer and his wife, Mr. and Mrs. Collins, did their best to make Rick feel at home. Shortly after supper Gus drove up. Working rapidly, he and Rick made the repairs and filled the tank. Rick returned to the farmhouse and Gus drove back to Whiteside.

"I'd like to get an early start," Rick told Mr. Collins, "and I'm afraid I'll have to have some of the grain cut so I can take off."

"We'll do that in the morning," the farmer said. "You just go on to bed. And don't worry about the price of the wheat either."

Rick was led to the room that Mrs. Collins had already prepared for him. He was exhausted and dropped wearily into the soft bed. Neither worry nor memories of the exciting day could keep him awake and soon he was asleep.

CHAPTER XV

The Man on the Cliff

SCOTTY walked through the silent Brant house and went noiselessly up the stairs to his room. All was quiet on Spindrift Island. Since returning to the island, he had made the rounds four times and had seen nothing to arouse his suspicions.

He put his gun on the bureau and stretched out on his bed, not to sleep, but to rest a for a little while. In about an hour he would get up and make the rounds again.

So far as he knew, everyone else on the island was sound asleep. After his talk with Hartson Brant, who had returned from New York, they had decided Scotty was the only one to be trusted as a guard, and that he should make the rounds hourly.

He closed his eyes and relaxed, wondering how Rick was making out. He had a mental picture of his friend trying to curl up in the cockpit of the little plane, or perhaps trying to get forty winks on the ground under a wing. Then he decided it was more likely that the farmer had provided him with a bed.

With the practiced ease that was the result of many nights of waiting in the jungle, he let his mind go blank.

The ticking of the clock on the bureau blended into his relaxed, half-asleep state, and he breathed rhythmically, content for the moment.

Suddenly he was fully alert again and staring up at the darkened ceiling, his whole body tense with listening. Some sound, too faint to be identified, had drifted in through the open window.

He swung out of bed noiselessly and glanced at the clock. The luminous dial told him it was just past four o'clock.

He stood at the window for long minutes, his eyes roving across the ground below.

A shadow moved through the orchard and was gone so swiftly he wasn't sure he hadn't imagined it; but he kept watching, alert for the slightest movement.

Then he saw the prowler.

A dark shape moved stealthily through the trees toward the back side of the island.

Scotty slipped his feet into moccasins Rick had given him. Then he hurried to the window again. The dark figure had vanished. Scotty guessed he was making for the woods beyond the laboratory.

The next moment, Scotty was swinging over the window sill. He didn't want to waste time going downstairs and through the house. He hung full length, then dropped.

Only a cricket broke the dark silence. He turned and went swiftly in the direction the prowler had taken. In a few moments the orchard was behind him and he stood in the clearing just outside the woods. He hesitated. Since he was going to the back of the island, he decided to go along the shore. The path wasn't so rough that way. He made his way along the seaward edge of the woods, watching for a sign of the prowler.

Suddenly he stopped short and turned sharply. A light had flickered, just for an instant, off in the woods to his right. There it was again, just for a second. The prowler was using a flashlight.

Somewhere over in that direction was the fork in the trail. Scotty estimated quickly. From what Rick had said, the tide would now be going out, giving easy access to the mainland. The prowler was taking this way to get off the island!

He put a hand on his hip and then withdrew it, berating himself for a fool. The pistol Mr. Brant had given him was back on his bureau. Forgetting the gun had made his problem much more difficult. He would have to get close and take the prowler by hand.

Once he had made the decision, he turned away from

the route the man had taken and hurried through the woods in a roundabout direction. He wanted to come out on the bluff overlooking the tidal flat.

His sense of direction steered him accurately. Other marines of his platoon had said that Scotty had "a compass in his head." Now that gift came in handy.

He reached the edge of the bluff and made his way along it, his ears attuned to every sound around him. But the prowler was making no noise. Suddenly Scotty dropped flat to the ground. A sixth sense had warned him that his quarry was only a few yards away, approaching the bluff from the trail.

On the open rim of the flats there was more light. He saw the dim figure come out of the trees to the rim of the ledge and halt; and at the same time, Scotty began to inch his way forward, his elbows and knees moving slowly.

The prowler was bent over, working at something Scotty couldn't see. He knew only that the vague silhouette had shortened as the man stooped over something on the ground.

He was holding his breath now and was moving with painful slowness. He had only a few feet to go; then he would rise with a piercing shout and charge. The yell would startle the prowler, and before he knew what was happening Scotty would be at him. He hoped grimly that the man wasn't good at infighting.

But even as the plan took form, Scotty froze, every muscle rigid. Lights had appeared on the New Jersey shore, powerful beams that swept over him and clicked off. There was the sound of an engine coming closer, then it coughed into silence.

Scotty lay still, hugging the ground. The prowler had confederates on the New Jersey shore. The dense woods had hidden the car and muffled the sound of its engine until it appeared at the very edge of the mainland shore.

But it was more than that! In the brief moment when the headlights had swept the bluff, Scotty had seen the prowler lowering something to the tidal flats by a rope!

CHAPTER XVI

Scotty Disappears

RICK awoke in the Collins farmhouse just after dawn. For a moment he didn't recognize the strange room; then, as the fog of sleep slipped away, he remembered and climbed quickly out of bed.

"My husband's clearing a path for your plane," Mrs. Collins told him. "Sit down and have some breakfast."

Rick looked longingly at the savory ham and eggs and thanked Mrs. Collins. Then he explained that he must get home as quickly as possible.

Mr. Collins was just finishing the path through the wheat when Rick arrived. He told the boy to forget about paying for the damage, but Rick wouldn't hear of it. He thanked the farmer and promised to send a check as soon as he got home.

There was a bad moment at the take-off when the Cub almost failed in the full-stall take-off, but Rick put the nose down and coaxed, and the small plane re-

sponded gallantly. He circled and waved to his watching host and then turned in the direction of Spindrift.

As the wheels touched turf on the island landing strip,
he mused, "I hope Scotty didn't dig up any trouble. Dad
should have gotten home last night. I hope Scotty told
him everything."

Hurrying out of the orchard toward the house, he
saw a familiar figure pacing the porch.

"Dad!" he called.

Hartson Brant came to meet him. "I was worried
about you, son. Glad to see you got back safely."

"I'm glad you're back, too, Dad," he said fervently.
"What about the microtron tube?"

Mr. Brant shook his head. "Vanished. Completely
vanished. And there's no doubt that it was stolen. I've
called the police again."

"We didn't do such a good job of handling things
while you were gone," Rick said disconsolately.

"It's not your fault."

"Then Scotty told you about what happened?"

Hartson Brant nodded. "Scotty kept watch last night;
but I'm afraid it was locking the barn after the horse
was stolen."

"Where is Scotty?" Rick asked.

"I haven't seen him this morning. I imagine he must
be at the laboratory. It's only seven o'clock, you know."

The two Brants walked toward the lab buildings and

found the place quiet. There was no sign of Scotty.

"He may be in his room," Mr. Brant suggested.

A feeling of apprehension crept over Rick. "I don't think so, Dad," he said, and ran toward the house.

There was no answer when he called Scotty's name, and his friend's room was empty. He ran back to the lab and searched again, without results.

"Scotty has disappeared," he told his father tensely.

"Are you sure?"

"He isn't around," Rick said. "There's no trace of him."

Mr. Brant's lips tightened. "First one of my associates turns traitor, and now this. If they've hurt that boy—"

"Dad," Rick interrupted, "here comes that detective again."

The police lieutenant who had left in such disgust a few days before was striding across the yard from the boat landing.

"Well, what is it this time?" was his greeting to Hartson Brant.

Rick's father told the detective about the missing microtron tube, and they walked toward the laboratories together.

"Scotty, where the heck are you?" Rick muttered to himself. He wasn't on the island, or he'd be at the house or lab. If he had been at the lab and had seen someone, he probably would have followed him. But where? To the mainland? Not by boat, because Rick had noticed that both boats were at the dock. There was only one other way to get off the island—the tidal flats.

There was no use bothering his father unless the idea produced something definite. He started on a run toward the back of the island.

Rick had not been a member of the Whiteside High School track team for nothing. In a few minutes he was breaking out of the woods into the clearing overlooking the flats.

The shelf of rock was deserted. If Scotty had chased anyone this far, he must have gone over the bluff. Rick went to the edge and looked down at the foam-flecked rocks below. It was past low tide and the water was rising again. As he turned back toward the path, he caught a flash of bright color to one side of the trail.

"Scotty!" he yelled, and ran toward the spot of blue.

It was Scotty's sweater! Rick reached for it, and as he did so, he felt something heavy, folded inside the garment. His breath caught sharply.

It was the microtron tube!

He stared around him unbelievingly, as though expecting Scotty to materialize out of nowhere and explain. Then he cradled the precious tube in both hands and ran for the laboratory.

Hartson Brant was just walking out of the building with the detective and John Stringfellow.

Mr. Brant saw the tube in Rick's hands. "Rick! Where did you find it?"

Stringfellow's jaw dropped.

"I found it at the flats in Scotty's sweater," Rick puffed.

"But how—" Stringfellow stopped. "How on earth did it get there?"

"Apparently Scotty put it there," Mr. Brant said. "The point is, where did he find it?"

"Doesn't it seem obvious to you, Hartson?" Stringfellow answered. "He stole it, found he couldn't get it off the island, and cached it in the woods."

"Scotty didn't steal it!" Rick leaped to his friend's defense. "But when we find him, we'll know who did, I bet!"

"Is this another one of those things?" the detective cut in dryly. "Can I go back to my little police station and have my nervous breakdown there?"

"You'd better stay, lieutenant," Hartson Brant said sharply. "That boy may return, and when he does, he is likely to have something to say that will interest you. It's ridiculous to think that he stole the tube. I suspect he took it away from someone."

Rick handed his father the tube, and in a few moments everyone on the island knew of its return.

"You may as well know," Hartson Brant announced to the staff, as they assembled in the main workroom, "that there is an effort being made to wreck this experiment. I do not know why this attempt is being made, but there is no doubt that it has been almost successful. We are on the last lap of our work now, and I have no doubt more serious steps may be taken to stop us. For that reason, I think we should have constant guards around the equipment. Lieutenant, will you call your office and provide for such guards?"

The detective nodded reluctantly. "I think you're seeing bogiemen," he said. "However, I'll do it."

As the scientists began to break up, to converse in low tones around the room, Rick went to the house for a belated breakfast. There was nothing he could do but wait for some word from Scotty.

To his surprise, his worries hadn't impaired his appetite and he ate heartily.

He was just buttering a piece of toast when he heard an odd hissing sound. A glance showed him Barby, standing just inside the living-room door, where Mrs. Brant could not see her.

Rick rose with studied casualness and walked to her side. Once out of earshot of his mother, he demanded: "What's up?"

Barby pointed to the telephone, breathless with excitement. "Scotty," she whispered.

Rick dived for the phone.

"Scotty, where the heck are you?"

"I've got them, Rick. Jump in the Cub and fly due West. I'll be waiting for you near the red steeple just outside of town. I'll wave my handkerchief. There's room to land."

"But what's it all about? Talk, Scotty!"

"Hold your hat," Scotty answered. "I've found the secret laboratory!"

CHAPTER XVII

The Secret Laboratory

WHEN Scotty saw the prowler lowering something over the bluff, he realized instantly what was happening. The man, whoever he was, had taken the stolen microtron tube from its hiding place and was putting it where his confederates could get it.

That put Scotty in a dilemma. If he rushed the prowler, the tube might be smashed in the struggle. If he didn't rush him, the man would get away, and he didn't want that. It was too good an opportunity to discover the identity of the traitor.

In a little while it would be dawn. Already the sky was more blue than black, but he could make out no details. There was nothing familiar about the prowler's vague silhouette.

He couldn't take the chance of breaking the fragile tube, he decided. He would have given much for a look at the traitor's face, but it wasn't to be risked. The tube came first.

He couldn't be sure whether the man was holding the end of the rope or whether he had tied it to something. If the man were waiting for his confederates to come and get the tube, he would have to risk an attack.

Then the prowler faded back into the woods and vanished, evidently wanting to get back to the Brant house before daylight. He had left the tube dangling where it could be found with ease.

Already Scotty could hear low voices from across the tidal flats. He had to act fast.

In a moment the object dangling over the bluff was in his hands—a small Boston bag. He jerked it open and his probing fingers touched rounded glass. The microtron tube!

He turned to run with it; then inspiration struck him. He took the fragile thing from the bag, hefting it in his hand. He felt around until he discovered a rock of the same approximate weight. He swiftly made the transfer and then lowered the bag back over the bluff.

He pulled off his sweater, and after carefully wrapping the tube in it, he hurried back along the path. He put the sweater a few feet off the trail. Rick would surely search for him, and he would almost certainly come down this path. He couldn't miss the bright blue of the sweater.

Excitement sang in his veins. What he was about to do would place him in the hands of the enemy, if they only knew it. But the chance he took might clear up the whole mystery. It was worth taking.

He went through the woods to the south side of the bluff, where the sea lapped softly against the island. He took off his clothes and made a bundle of them; then he slid into the water, holding the garments high.

The water was fairly calm, but the tide pulled at him. He circled wide, away from the rocks of the tidal flat and into deep water. He reached the mainland and dressed swiftly. Then he felt his way through the wooded coast line, until the faint gleam of starlight on glass told him he had reached the car. It was, as he had expected, the gray sedan.

He stood under a sheltering clump of birch, tensely listening. Minutes ticked by and he heard no sound. He had given the tidal flats a wide berth in his swim to the mainland; they had not seen him. At last, satisfied, he hurried to the car, approaching it cautiously from the rear.

It was deserted. Its occupants were probably picking up the Boston bag right now. If they opened the bag . . . But he didn't believe they would. They would be in a hurry to get clear before the morning light gave them away. Already it was growing lighter.

The trunk of the car was locked. He tested the handle gingerly and then jerked with all his strength, wincing as the compartment snapped open. Then, with sweat starting out on his forehead, he crawled in and let the door swing shut. It closed with a rasp of the hinges and almost locked before he realized there would be no way of getting out again.

Straining to reach his hip pocket in the cramped space, he took his handkerchief and wadded it under the locking bolt. Now the door would be almost closed, but not locked. He blessed the luck that had made the lock the easily sprung kind.

His shoulder rested against a spare tire that gouged into his side, and his knees were drawn up almost to his chin. He wished for a moment that he had gone straight home with the tube. Every time the sedan hit a bump, he would crash against all the projections in the luggage compartment. He'd be lucky if he had any skin left when the ride was over.

It was agony to lie perfectly still. Something ground into his ankle. He tried to reach it, but there wasn't room to shift his shoulders so he could move his arm. After a few tries he lay still, suffering in silence.

The compartment blanketed sound. The men were opening the car doors before he knew they had arrived. The engine roared into life and he knew any slight noise he might make would go unheard. He tried to shift into a more comfortable position.

The car lurched and his head came into violent contact with a metal projection. He stifled a gasp of pain and clutched his head in both hands. When the pain subsided a little, he squirmed around until he was slightly more comfortable; then he held on grimly. Whatever road the sedan was traveling seemed to have been chosen for the number of bumps in it.

A new discomfort crowded in on him—hot, fume-filled air. He stood it as long as he could and then pushed the compartment door slightly open. A brown, dirt road flashed by under the car and he knew they had not yet reached the main highway.

It was light outside. Now and then the sedan passed a clearing in the woods and he could see it was almost day. He resigned himself to choking on gasoline fumes and accepted the various jolts and bumps as stoically as he could.

If the ride took him nearer a solution of the Brants' troubles, it would be worth the discomforts. Scotty felt a strong sense of obligation to the Brants as well as a deep liking for them. They had taken him off the road and accepted him as one of them.

The bumping gave way to a smooth drone of tires and he knew they were on paved road at last. A kind of drowsiness overtook him, born of the close, fume-filled air, the soothing hum of tires, and of his lack of sleep. When the car swerved suddenly into another dirt road, he was almost asleep. A bad jounce roused him painfully, raising another lump on his battered head.

The car swung in a slow circle and stopped.

While he waited, hardly daring to breathe, there was the creak of a metal door opening. The car rolled forward again, but only a few yards. He heard the car doors slam shut.

The engine was silent now, and he could hear the muffled conversation of two men, but he couldn't make out the words. The sound died with the closing of another door and he knew he was alone.

Slowly he raised the compartment door, breathing in fresh air gratefully. He unwound his cramped body and stepped out, poised for instant flight.

He stood on the floor of a large, barnlike structure that had been a factory of some sort. Now the metal beams were rusted and the floor was littered with odds and ends. On both sides of the car, window-studded walls rose to a height of three stories.

He guessed he was in what had once been a loading room between the two wings of the factory. The rest of the plant was behind those windowed walls.

A near-by door attracted him and he went to it, silent in his moccasins. He tried the handle and the door gave easily. He pushed a little, peering through as the door swung open. A long deserted hallway stretched before him. He went down it, passing what had been a large machine shop, with rusted lathe beds still bolted to the floor. Then he was in the midst of deserted offices.

The end of the hallway loomed, with no trace of the men, and he stood there, uncertain. Where had they gone? He tried a near-by door and it gave onto a flight of stairs.

Scotty's heart hammered heavily as he went up, keeping close to the wall. It was possible to avoid creaks in the old stairs if one kept close to the edge. His marine training had taught him that.

The top of the stairs opened onto another hallway. This time he heard angry voices from a room at the end. He hugged the wall, his spine tingling as though ice cubes were forming there. If they saw him . . .

A small room, its door open, attracted him. He slipped into it and looked around. It was empty. There was a small closet. And in one blank wall was a window.

He went to the window silently. It was cut so that tools could be passed through—the room he was in probably had been used as a toolroom. He looked through the window and dodged back, sweat starting out on his forehead. He had looked into an enormous room two stories high, in which four men stood. They were the men who had been at the old barn.

Looking through the window was risky. He searched and found a series of holes that led into the big room, probably drilled to hold bolts for some since-removed shelving. He applied his eye to one and had a clear view of the four men. They were standing around a table on which the Boston bag lay open, and they were arguing heatedly.

"A rock," a strident voice was saying, "a crummy rock! What's the matter with that guy, boss?"

"There has been some mistake. I don't know how it happened, but I intend to find out." The commanding voice must be that of Scarface. "And if we have been double-crossed, we will know what to do."

"I ought to beat his head in," the first voice growled.

"That would be foolish," Scarface said. "Don't forget, we must have his help."

"Well, what are we waiting for? Let's go find out." That was the bearded man, the one he had heard called Carlos when they were at the barn.

"Yeah. While you find out about this rock deal, boss, I'm gonna get some grub. I don't like this gettin' up before breakfast."

"We will eat," Scarface said, "after I have made a telephone call to . . ."

Scotty strained his ears to catch the name, but one of the men chose that moment to knock something off the table with a crash.

"What rotten luck!" the boy muttered under his breath. The men were walking to the door now. He hurried to the closet and stepped inside, swinging the door shut.

Footsteps passed down the hallway and he heard

the men go down the stairs. In a few moments the car roared into life and backed out onto the gravel road.

Scotty walked out of his hiding place and into the big room. He knew nothing of electronics, but he knew radio gear when he saw it. The place was full of racks containing tubes and intricate wiring, and in one corner was a tall cyclinder of gleaming metal.

"The laboratory!" he exulted. "This is it!"

He hurried to the window and looked out through the dirty panes, trying to orient himself. Nothing but woods stretched out below him. On the other side of the building, though, he saw houses, and a few hundred yards away, a church with a red steeple.

The next step was to call Rick. His friend would be worried about his absence—if he had found out about it yet, for it was still early.

He left the supposedly abandoned factory and trudged down the road to the settlement beyond. With the discovery of the secret lab, he thought, a lot of questions were on the point of being answered.

CHAPTER XVIII

Captured!

RICK followed Scotty from the field near the red steeple, where he had landed his Cub. They plunged into the woods. As they walked, Scotty outlined the events of the few hours preceding. Soon they were near the road leading to the old factory, and as they reached the road, Rick saw the building.

"No wonder we didn't spot that from the air," he remarked. "I never thought of looking so close to town."

"We'd better work fast," Scotty advised. "I don't think they'll be gone long."

Rick stopped. "Work fast at what?" he said. "Now that we've found the place, what can we do about it?"

Scotty scratched his head. "Gosh, I didn't think of that. We can't carry it away, can we?"

"No, all we can do is look around to make sure this is the secret lab, and then notify Dad. Let's go."

Scotty led Rick to the factory and then to the room where the four men had been.

Rick looked around with eyes wide open. "Brother, did you find the *laboratory* all right!" he said. He made a quick inspection of the equipment that littered the room. He stopped at a complicated arrangement of wires and dials. "It's an exact copy of our control panel at Spindrift."

"In fact, the whole place looks like a copy of your dad's lab," Scotty said. "Only not as clean."

"It's fantastic," Rick said. "But here it is."

"Look! The rocket itself!" Scotty exclaimed, pointing toward the end of the big laboratory. "Part of it anyway. The rest must be somewhere else. It's not in this building."

Rick probed into the interior of the control panel, noting that the wiring was neatly done, evidently by a technician of high training and experience. The separate wires were tied together to form cables and they were tied tight by a series of half hitches. Rick stared at them for a moment, unable to tell why those little loops seemed so familiar to him.

He was still looking at the wiring, lost in thought, when Scotty grabbed his arm in warning.

"A car just drove in!" he gasped.

"The gang!" Rick whispered. "Now we're in for it!"

Scotty's eyes were racing around the room, looking

desperately for a hiding place. "Over here!" he said.

They ran to the rocket cylinder and crouched behind it. "Not very good," Rick said shakily. "They'll spot us for sure."

"I know," Scotty answered tautly. "But it's the only thing in the room to hide behind. If we try to leave, we'll bump right into them."

They heard the sound of footsteps on the stairs. Soon three men walked into the room. Rick felt dampness spring out on his forehead.

One of the thugs was saying "How do we know this guy on the island ain't givin' us the old double cross?"

"Don't be stupid!" the bearded man said irritably. "Without us, what good does the tube do him?"

Rick knew that the "him" the men were talking about was the Spindrift Island traitor, and he prayed that they would mention his name.

"Kogan," the bearded man continued, "we must continue work on the rocket. Get your tools."

The two boys tensed. They were hiding behind the rocket and the men were going to work on it.

Scotty nudged him. "Well, get ready," he said softly.

Rick's legs flexed and he rose to a half crouch. He didn't know whether Scotty meant to run or fight—and there wasn't time to ask. Footsteps advanced toward their hiding place. "Bring your soldering iron," the bearded man said, his voice almost above them, "we'll solder the connections to the intermediate stage."

A foot scraped only inches from Rick's head and the sweat rolled in driblets down his chin. They had to discover them, and any second now.

"I have the crystal," the voice went on. "First we will—" He stopped, biting off the word.

This was it.

With fist poised, Scotty sprang to his feet and charged. He drove his arm forward, straight at Kogan's stomach. The man went down and Scotty yelled, "Come on!"

Rick sprinted hard behind his pal, across the room. They bowled over the bearded man and shot straight for the door. But the third man had anticipated the move and was waiting for them.

The thug caught up a piece of pipe and poised it as Scotty ran toward him. Rick caught his breath as he saw the length of pipe arch up, but Scotty feinted with his feet to draw a swing from the man and then, as the pipe swished harmlessly by, floored him with one punch.

"Beat it!" he yelled, and headed for the door. But before they had taken two steps, a voice rang out behind them.

"Stop, or I fire!" It was the bearded man. In his hand was an ugly pistol—a Luger. It looked big as the end of a water main as it was shifted from Scotty to Rick.

"That's better," the man said calmly. He paused. "So we meet again, young Brant?" The pistol muzzle traveled to Scotty. "And this, I believe, is your rescuer."

Rick and Scotty said nothing.

"Felsen, get up and search them!"

There was the sound of footsteps behind Rick, then hot breath on his neck as hands patted his clothes, then Scotty's, searching for weapons.

"They're clean," the thug said.

The next order was cold—unemotional. "Get some rope."

"A pleasure," said the man named Kogan. "Let me beat their heads in with it!"

"The rope. Quickly," snapped the bearded man.

The boys watched Kogan walk toward a cabinet and take out the rope. The pistol muzzle still wandered from one to the other.

"How co-operative of you to place yourselves in our hands this way!" the man holding the Luger said. "Kidnaping was to be our last resort, but you will admit it is an effective way of making your father give up his little experiment, eh?"

Rick pressed his lips together, but did not answer. He knew how right the man was. The other scientists on Spindrift might keep on working, but without Hartson Brant's guiding genius, they would most certainly lose out in the race for the Stoneridge grant.

"Do not be afraid," Carlos said. "It is not in my mind to harm you. When the experiment is concluded, you will be set free. Meanwhile you will make excellent hostages. With Brant worrying about the safety of his precious son, I do not think we need fear the success of the people on the island."

"When we get out of here," Scotty threatened, "we'll have the FBI on your trail so fast it'll make your head spin!"

Carlos was unperturbed. He glanced up as Kogan approached with the rope. "Nice, tight knots, my dear Kogan," he said, and stepped back so the man could do his job.

It was senseless to struggle. Rick submitted quietly as his arms and legs were bound. A line was passed between his ankles, and his legs were trussed up and brought close to his wrists behind him. When the trussing was done, he lay on the floor, unable to move without sending waves of pain through his limbs.

Scotty was somewhere behind him. He tried to twist, to see his friend, but a warning foot pressed against him. "Relax," Felsen said.

At an order from Carlos, they were picked up and carried to a corner of the big room. There was a door there that they hadn't noticed. It was open, revealing a small room, bare of any furniture.

Carlos stood over them. "Don't attempt to escape,"

he snapped. "There will be a guard here every moment." The door slammed.

The wall was thin. The boys could hear Carlos giving further orders.

"It will not be safe to keep them here. Felsen, you and I will go to the other place and prepare it. Kogan will guard them. We will be back in time to see the boss," he went on. "He would not like it if they escaped."

There was a grunt from Kogan, and the boys heard footsteps moving toward the door. It slammed and a few moments later a car started and faded away on the road.

Scotty spoke first. "I can't move my hands. Can you, Rick?"

Rick tried to flex his arms and legs. They wouldn't give an inch. "No," he said. "We're tied for good."

He heard Scotty grunting as though fighting his bonds and then there was silence.

"It was my fault," he said finally.

"It was no one's fault," Rick answered. "We were just unlucky. A few more minutes and we would have been in the clear."

"Well, what do we do now?"

"Got some checkers on you?" Rick asked wryly.

The guard, Kogan, hammered at the door. "Pipe down in there!"

"All right," Scotty yelled back. "We won't say a word. We're mad at each other anyway!"

Rick was amazed at the outburst. Then something touched him from behind, and he realized his friend had yelled to cover the slight noise of his body moving across the floor. Scotty had managed to squirm close.

"Shut up, or I'll come in and shut you up," Kogan called.

"I'm shut!" Scotty retorted.

He fell silent. Then Rick was conscious of a tugging at his bonds. Scotty was gnawing at the ropes with his teeth, trying to loosen the knot!

Time stretched on interminably. Rick turned his head but he was unable to see Scotty. Gazing at the ceiling, he noticed the wiring for the lights and decided it had been tacked on as an afterthought. A single bulb hung from a cord in the center of the room.

The movement behind him ceased. He squirmed around until he was face to face with Scotty. His friend smiled at him through swollen lips. "Turn back again," he whispered. "I was just resting."

Rick obediently turned around again. It was an eternity before Scotty whispered, "Pull hard." Rick put all his strength into jerking his legs straight and then he felt something give.

"That's enough," Scotty whispered.

The guard pounded on the door and Rick gave a startled jerk. At that moment, the rope parted and his hands were free.

"What are you doing in there?" Kogan demanded.

"Thinking!" Scotty yelled. "Do you want us to start talking again?"

"Don't be a wise guy," Kogan answered. "Or you'll wish you hadn't been." They heard his chair scrape as he resumed his seat outside the door.

Rick rubbed life into his hands and swiftly unbound his legs. In a moment, Scotty's bonds fell to the floor and they sat up, grinning at each other.

"Let's take a look," Scotty said.

They crawled to the single window on hands and knees. At the sill, they rubbed a space in the pane clear and looked down.

Scotty shook his head. They were two stories up, and the factory was situated on a hill that dropped away sharply under them. It was too far to the ground for a jump.

"That's that," Rick whispered.

Scotty nodded.

"There must be some way out."

Scotty pointed toward the door. "There is," he said. "If only we could get Kogan to open that door."

Rick sat down on the floor, rubbing his legs where the rope had cut. Kogan didn't know they were unbound. If only he would open the door wide enough for them to rush him, it would be two against one.

"He must have a gun," Scotty said.

"He might not fire," Rick whispered. "They aren't out to kill us."

Scotty grinned mirthlessly. "I don't want to be the one to find out."

They had been talking in whispers, but, inadvertently, Rick had raised his voice.

"Quiet in there!" Kogan bellowed.

"Quiet yourself, knucklehead!" Rick retorted.

Scotty stared his amazement.

"Try to make him angry," Rick urged. "He may tell us whether or not he has the gun."

Scotty raised his voice instantly. "Come in here and untie one hand, muttonhead. I want to see if your skull's as thick as it looks."

The guard shouted, "I'll give you one more chance. Keep quiet, or I'll come in there and gag you!"

"Come on," Scotty jeered. "Come on in, Kogan. Aren't you lonesome out there?"

Rick joined in. "Keep us quiet if you can, Kogan." He let out a wild yell.

The harsh voice waited until the yell died away. Then it spoke, quietly ominous. "One more yip out of either of you and I blast a couple of slugs through the door."

The boys' eyes met.

"Now we know," Scotty said.

Somewhere far away, a dog barked. Rick stirred rest-

lowed, "I've got it! It's that kid's dog. I've seen him at the airport. Listen, who are you?"

"Why," Barby faltered, "I—that is, I—"

"You look like him," Kogan said ominously. "Wait a minute, don't get too close to that door. Just move over to the other side of the room, sister."

"I think I'd better be going," Barby said. There was sudden fright in her voice. "Come on, Diz."

"You ain't goin' anywhere." Kogan sounded sure of himself.

Rick could almost read the guard's thoughts: Scarface would have only high praise and perhaps a reward if Kogan captured his sister.

"Please let me go!" Barby sounded terrified now.

"Don't be in a hurry," Kogan said. "Come on. Don't try to run, now. Ow!" He let out a bellow. "Kick me in the shins, would you?"

Scotty's solid frame smashed against the door. It wouldn't budge. He whirled to Rick, a wild look in his eyes. "We've got to get out!"

Rick heard Barby's scream of fright, and on the instant, he left the floor in a wild leap, his hand upstretched to the dangling light fixture. His hand just brushed it—he missed. He fell back to the floor.

"I'll get it," he said through clenched teeth. He crouched, then shot ceilingward again. His hand closed around the socket and held fast. The jerk almost dislocated his arm, but the wiring yielded and he landed in a heap on the floor, the socket in his hands.

Scotty grabbed the loose wiring and threw his weight on it. It ripped loose and tumbled in a mass to the floor. Then he and Rick combined their weights in a jerk that snapped the wires loose from the junction box high overhead.

Rick took the socket end of the wire and wound it around his waist twice.

Scotty ran to the window and crashed his foot through it, kicking at the broken pane until it was free of jagged edges.

From outside the door they heard the sound of running feet and Kogan's yell to Barby to stop before she got hurt. Rick took the wire in both hands and lay flat on the floor, his feet braced against the wall under the window.

Scotty was out the window in an instant, and there were long seconds when the wire bit cruelly into Rick's body and scored deep lines across his hands. Then the wire went slack and he rose, pulling it from around him. He ran to the door and put his ear against it.

"Those kids are getting away," Kogan shouted. "Don't move, you!"

Feet pounded toward the door. The guard had heard the window shatter. Rick bent low, ready to rush him.

The key grated in the door. The moment daylight

showed through, his shoulder smashed into the panel.

The door crunched into something solid and he heard a muffled grunt from Kogan, then he was through the opening, sprawling headlong with the force of his rush.

"Rick!" Barby screamed.

He managed to catch a glimpse of her, behind the rocket cylinder, before he whirled to face Kogan just as the guard pulled the Luger from his pocket. Rick started forward and the pistol muzzle steadied on a direct line with his head.

"Don't try it," Kogan said harshly.

Rick stopped, breathing hard.

The guard got to his feet, the pistol unwavering on Rick's head. "Where's the other one?"

"He flew out the window," Rick answered. "Just like a little bird. And he'll be back with the cops."

A slim hand slipped into his. He turned and managed a smile for a very frightened Barby. "It's all right, sis," he said. "He won't do anything."

Dismal trotted over and whined a greeting. Rick bent and fondled his ears, listening for any sound from Scotty. Was he imagining things or had he heard the soft scrape of footsteps just outside the door?

Kogan gestured with the pistol. "Back against the wall, both of you. And don't make a false move, or I'll blast you."

Rick gasped as Barby took a step toward the guard. "You wouldn't dare," she said defiantly.

Kogan's hand lifted menacingly, and in that moment Dismal decided to take a hand.

With a low snarl, the little dog leaped for the man who was menacing his young mistress. His teeth clamped firmly into Kogan's leg and he held on.

Rick started forward, but Scotty was quicker. He came across the room in a mad rush and his shoulder battered into Kogan's midriff. The gun flew across the room and the guard went backward. His head crashed against the wall. He jerked once and slid to the floor, unconscious.

Scotty turned to Barby. "Are you all right?" he asked anxiously.

The girl nodded, eyes wide. "Where did you come from?"

"I was waiting outside the door. Thanks to Diz, I got a chance to do something."

"Let's get out of here," Rick said urgently.

"Just a minute." Scotty picked up the Luger. He leveled it at the unfinished control section of the rocket, and orange flame spurted from the muzzle. The crash of the shot sounded in Rick's ears, followed by the tinkle of glass.

Four times more, Scotty pressed the trigger. Then, not content with the damage he had done, he went to the cylinder and reversed the pistol, hammering with the butt until the delicate mechanism was a tangled mass of torn wiring and broken tubes.

"Let them repair that," he said grimly. "Come on, kids. Let's get out of here."

Rick kept a firm grip on Barby's hand. He shook his head at the fury in Scotty's face. It was the first time he had ever seen his friend really angry. He hoped Carlos and the others wouldn't return. Scotty was in a mood to shoot straight and fast.

Outside the building, Scotty turned to them, and his face was its usually friendly self. "I don't like mugs who try to put their hands on girls," he said. "It makes me lose my temper."

"Were you angry?" Rick said grinning weakly. "I wouldn't have known."

"Stop it, Rick," Barby commanded. "I think Scotty was wonderful!"

CHAPTER XIX

Rick's Gadget Works

HARTSON BRANT paced the floor of the living room before Rick, Barby, and Scotty. They sat on the floor, while Dismal, the hero of the day, sat enthroned in the chair.

"You might have been killed," Rick's father said, "chasing off after those men like that!"

"But it had to be done, Dad," Rick pointed out. "And we have the goods on them now."

"Have you?" Hartson Brant stopped his pacing and looked at his son. "I'm not so sure. You found the laboratory, yes. But having a lab isn't illegal. Those men might even be able to squeeze out of holding you prisoner. Didn't you trespass? And didn't you smash their equipment?"

"But they shot at the plane," Rick protested. "And they tried to force me down with that stolen biplane."

"Even those things would be hard to prove," Hartson

172

Brant said, "unless we can find out the name of the traitor."

"I have some ideas, Dad," Rick said thoughtfully. "First, the messages on the barn. We know now that they were written with special paint. We know it took special lenses to read the messages. If we could find those lenses, that would tell us something."

"Do you think the traitor would leave them lying around?" Hartson Brant asked dryly. "And there's one thing we haven't considered. Even if we catch the traitor, we still won't have the top man."

"Why couldn't the traitor be the top man?" Rick was puzzled.

"We must assume that they are trying to wreck our experiment in order to leave a clear field for a rocket of their own. Evidently, through this traitor, they have kept abreast of our developments, planning to use our knowledge to complete their own rocket. That means they are after the Stoneridge grant of two million dollars."

"That's right, Dad," Rick agreed. "I can't think of any other answer."

"The traitor could not apply for the grant in his own name, don't you see? The fact that he had been working with me would point the finger of guilt at him immediately. That means the gang is led by an outsider, a scientist with some reputation. The traitor and the others are mere hirelings, working for a share of the two million."

Scotty spoke up. "Couldn't Scarface be the leader, sir?"

"I have never known a man such as you describe," Hartson Brant said. "And I know every scientist working in this field. No, I'm afraid the identity of the top man is still a secret."

"We should certainly have those men picked up, though," Rick suggested. "The police could get them when they return to the factory."

"I'll phone immediately." Hartson Brant walked out to the switchboard to call the Whiteside State Police.

"There's one thing you haven't explained, Barby," Rick said. "How on earth did you wind up at the factory?"

"Well," Barby answered, "I listened in while you were talking to Scotty. When you didn't come back right away, I thought you were having some fun Dismal and I should get in on, so we took a boat and went over. I never dreamed—"

"I guess you didn't," Rick said.

Scotty suddenly snapped his fingers. "The love letter. We forgot about that."

"I didn't," Rick said. "Anyway, Jerry has it. I doubt that it will tell us much."

"That code stops me," Scotty remarked. "And why

did they change the sign from 'Smoke' to 'Drink' and back again?"

"I think it was to tell the traitor there was a message for him," Rick said. "He couldn't take the chance of being seen looking through binoculars every day, and that way he would just have to look at the barn and see if there was a message. If so, he could get the glasses. There was no danger of anyone's noticing the word change except for aircraft, and then only if a fellow flew over it every day, as I did."

"That was where they slipped," Scotty agreed.

"If only we could find the traitor with those lenses on him, or find them in his room."

"Well, why don't we try?"

Hartson Brant came in at that moment. "Try what?"

"To find the lenses, Dad," Rick explained. "We can search for them while all the men are at the lab, if you'll try to keep them there."

Mr. Brant considered. "I don't like it. But I suppose there's no other way. I'm going to the lab right now. The police will be here shortly."

"Just a minute, Dad," Rick said suddenly, "I've been wanting to ask you. How does it happen that everyone on the staff has a copy of *Psychiatry Simplified?* That was the code book, you know."

"It was clever of our man, whoever he is, to use that book. Dr. Judson Chambers, the author, is an old friend. He sent us all autographed copies."

"I wish there had been some other explanation," Rick said. "It might have given us a clue."

"Concentrate on finding the lenses," Mr. Brant said. "I'll go along to the lab."

Rick posted Barby at the front door with instructions to run and warn them if anyone came from the lab and then he and Scotty went to the long corridor from which branched the combination bedrooms and offices of the scientists.

Again Rick felt guilt at prowling through the belongings of men whom he respected and liked; but, as his father had said, there was no other way.

Weiss's room was the first stop. "Look everywhere," he told Scotty. He reached for a desk drawer and began searching. As he inspected the last drawer, he noticed the curled bit of scotch tape stuck to the edge.

"Scotty, Weiss wasn't lying," he said, indicating the tape.

"Then he did try to trap the traitor."

"Yes, but don't forget he's the only one besides Dad who has binoculars," Rick reminded him.

"We've never seen him use them," Scotty pointed out. "And they're not here now."

"And neither are the lenses," Rick said.

They moved to the next room.

"Zircon's," he said.

"We saw him reading the key book to the code, remember?"

"But everyone else has a copy, too, so that's nothing against him."

"Lenses would be, if we could find them," Scotty commented.

Rick went through the desk, while Scotty searched the other furniture in the room.

"Nothing," Rick said as they finished. "That leaves only one more place."

They went down the corridor and into the last scientist's quarters.

"Look!" Scotty exclaimed as they closed the door.

There, on top of a bookcase, were Weiss's binoculars.

"Now," Rick said excitedly, "if only the lenses are here, too!"

They searched the big room twice before giving up, refusing to believe the lenses would not be in this last place. Then Rick dropped into a chair. "No luck," he said. "We're sunk, Scotty."

"And right up there are the very glasses used to read those messages," Scotty said unhappily. "I'm sure of it. If only the lenses were with them!" He reached idly for the glasses.

Rick sat bolt upright. "Let me see those."

He flicked a finger over the end of the binoculars, right where the lens mounts were fitted. "Does this metal look scratched to you?"

"No, but the lens mounts look newer than the rest."

"Maybe they've been painted recently." Rick

scratched at the paint covering and, to his amazement, a large flake came loose, disclosing older paint underneath. "They *have* been painted," he said. "Do you think new lenses have been added?"

"Holy smoke!" Scotty exclaimed. "Do you think this is what we've been looking for?"

"They must be," Rick said. "But why couldn't I read a message on the barn when I looked through them?"

Scotty shook his head. "I don't know."

"Wait! I've got it!" Rick ran from the room with Scotty close behind. Down the stairs they went and across the orchard. Rick headed for the tidal flats, sprinting as fast as he could go.

They brought up at the bluff, a little breathless, and Rick put the glasses to his eyes. The barn came into focus, and the sign. "Scotty," he choked, "look!"

Scotty took the glasses and held them on the sign.

There, in blue letters against the white of the sign, was the message:

BEAT IT!

"Don't you see?" Rick said. "When we caught Stringfellow here, the sign said 'Drink White Cream,' which was the normal reading. There was no message then!"

"Then why did he have the glasses trained on it," Scotty objected.

"I don't know for sure, but if he were the one who dropped the radiation shields, he'd have suffered from a slight burn that could have affected his eyes. Besides, he missed a lot of sleep. Maybe he couldn't see the sign without the glasses."

"Sounds reasonable," Scotty answered. "But there would have been a message left on the sign from the day before."

"The paint is special stuff," Rick said. "Maybe the chemical evaporates in a few hours. The cans were tightly covered, remember. That way, they could repaint almost every day without painting over the old numbers, because they'd have faded. Remember, we didn't hear them painting out an old message."

"Then it's Stringfellow!" Scotty declared.

"Right," Rick said grimly. "He's the one who sold us out for a cut of that two million."

They ran back to the laboratory, and as they reached the door, they could see the scientists inside, working on the final stages of the moon rocket.

Hartson Brant came to them as they entered.

Rick hesitated. "How are things going, Dad?"

"If nothing more happens," Mr. Brant replied, "we should be able to launch on schedule tomorrow night."

"Nothing more will happen," Rick said, and he looked straight at Stringfellow. "We've found the traitor, Dad."

Stringfellow came to his feet, startled. "Who is it?" he asked huskily.

Rick took the binoculars from behind his back. "Do these answer your question?"

A faint trace of alarm appeared in Stringfellow's eyes, but he was immediately composed again. "No, I don't think they do."

"We read the secret message on the barn," Rick snapped. "Your friends have flown the coop. They've left you holding the bag."

"I haven't the faintest idea of what you're talking about," Stringfellow said icily.

"Rick!" Hartson Brant said. "What is all this?"

"I just remembered," Rick explained, "that it was Stringfellow who was standing at the tail of my plane the day I went to Newark. He was the one who put the message in the tail. Only, his friends at the airport didn't get it, and neither did Mac in the black plane."

"Hartson, would you mind telling me what this is all about?" Stringfellow demanded.

"I will tell you," Hobart Zircon cut in. "I remember now that it was *you* who told *me* that the lock on the shields was broken, not the other way around. You were arranging a reason for the shields being down, but I never saw it until now!"

"Of course not," Rick said. "Besides, that shields thing was an accident."

All faces turned to Rick.

"He was trying to steal the microtron that night, only

he heard us coming, and the shields crashed open because he was in a hurry to get away. He didn't have time to put them back up. The next night, he got the tube."

Stringfellow turned white. "Do you realize what you are accusing me of?"

"About every crime in the book," Rick said. "Including shooting us down. Wasn't that because one of the thugs lost his head? I think that field was the place where you were going to erect your own rocket launcher!"

A gray look crept over Stringfellow's features. His eyes went to the door.

"Do any of you know this guy?" Rick heard the detective's voice say.

Rick wheeled. The burly detective was holding a young man in a sports coat and turned-up hat squarely by the scruff of the neck.

"Jerry Webster!" Rick shouted. "Am I glad to see you!"

"No gladder than I," Jerry said, wrenching free from the relaxed grip of the detective. "Every time I pay you a visit I get manhandled." He held out his hand with a folded slip of paper. "Here's your love letter."

Rick grabbed for the decoded note. His eyes swept the sheet and he turned to his father.

"Listen to this, Dad," he said. " 'The experiment is being delayed to the best of my ability. I will try to steal the tube at my first opportunity. This should delay them until we can complete our work.' " Rick paused. "Signed, 'J. S.'—John Stringfellow!"

"John Stringfellow," Hartson Brant repeated huskily, his unbelieving eyes on the man he had trusted.

Rick's moment of triumph gave way to unhappiness. He saw the hurt disbelief in Hartson Brant's face and knew his father was deeply shaken at this overwhelming evidence of Stringfellow's guilt.

All eyes had turned to Hartson Brant, and Stringfellow was quick to take advantage of the brief, unguarded moment.

The thin scientist made a dive for a drawer in his workbench. Before anyone could reach him he wrenched the drawer open and grabbed a .45 automatic.

"I'll blow a hole through the first man who makes a move," he said coldly. "I'm going through that door and out of here."

Every eye turned to the detective who stood squarely in the middle of the door. Rick saw a little muscle near his temple flick and swell.

"Then you'll have to go through the hole you blow in me," the detective said tensely. "Come on."

It was a battle of eyes between Stringfellow and the detective. "I don't want to hurt anyone," the thin-faced man warned in a hoarse voice, "but if I must, I will."

Every man in the room could see that the slightest hostile move from any of them would cause Stringfellow's finger to constrict on the trigger.

"If you won't move from that door, I'll go out the back way," he said. "Don't follow me beyond that spot." He nodded to a bench separating him from the others.

Slowly he began to back toward a side door. On the bench behind the scientist lay the electrical shock machine which Rick had constructed and laid so carelessly on the bench. He was thinking.

The scientist felt his way slowly, ever so slowly, to the bench. Rick's arm stole out toward the wire that trailed from the electrical device. If only he could reach the button in time.

Stringfellow's back bumped into the metal bench. With a wild grab, Rick reached for the button and pushed it. A cry of alarm came from Stringfellow's lips as the electric current shot through him. In the split second when his gun bobbed in the air, Scotty hurled himself across the room, directly against the scientist's legs.

Down they went, the man swinging wildly with the butt of the automatic. But a stunning left smashed against Stringfellow's mouth and a roundhouse right landed against his jaw.

With a moan of pain, the thin-faced man collapsed in

a heap under Scotty's attack. The youth drew back his fist to strike again but Rick yelled, "No! He's done for, Scotty."

In a moment, everyone crowded to the boys' side, all asking how they had trapped Stringfellow. Hartson Brant put both arms around their shoulders and squeezed hard.

"Every man in this room owes you a debt he cannot repay," he said, blinking strangely.

CHAPTER XX

A Great Day for Spindrift

RICK slept soundly that night. The State Police, acting instantly after Hartson Brant's call, had gone to the secret lab and rounded up the gang. Even Mac, the missing airport attendant, had been caught. Only Scarface had slipped through the police net, and he was sure to be picked up within a short time, the lieutenant said.

There was a great crowd gathered at the breakfast table when Rick went downstairs next morning. The scientists who had been vacationing had reassembled for the final experiment. Rick greeted them, glad to see all the familiar faces once more.

A man with freshly shaven face and amused eyes called from the end of the table as the boys sat down. "I hear you've been studying to be a detective instead of a wire mechanic, Rick." He was Dr. Wisecarver who had helped develop the rocket fuel.

"I wish you'd tell me the secret of those inches you've

185

grown since the start of the summer," said a very short and smiling scientist. This was Professor Gordon who had designed the rocket launcher.

With everyone excited and in a gay mood, breakfast was noisy and amusing. Even Zircon and Weiss had recovered from last night's events and were their jovial selves again.

Looking from the window, Rick could see a crowd of men gathering. There were reporters by the score and men unloading broadcast equipment from sound trucks. The newsreel men were setting up their cameras to get pictures of the proceedings from start to finish.

"It's a great day for you and your dad," Scotty said.

"And it almost didn't happen." Rick smiled. "It might not have happened if you hadn't been around at the right time."

"I'll bet old Scarface is still running," Scotty remarked.

"I certainly hope so," Rick said seriously.

Scotty nodded his readiness to leave, and the two boys rose from the table and strolled into the big yard.

"Say, Jerry Webster ought to be in this gang of reporters," Rick said. "Let's look for him."

They began meandering through the crowd of reporters and guests, trying to find the young reporter.

"Funny he didn't come looking for me," Rick commented. He saw Professor Zircon talking to a group of dignified-looking visitors and headed his way.

"Excuse me, Professor Zircon," Rick said. "Didn't you drive the speedboat over to pick up the reporters?"

"Why, yes," the professor answered.

"Did you see Jerry Webster? You remember. The young reporter who was dragged into the laboratory yesterday—the one with the note."

Zircon rubbed his beard thoughtfully. "No, I don't believe I saw his face in the boat," he said. "Wait. I have the list of reporters here. They all had to show passes and sign this list."

He reached for a list of names on a near-by table. Rick peered over his shoulder.

"Yes! There's his name," Rick said when he came to it. He pointed to the name Jerry Webster, which was written in a flourishing script.

"Well, he's here then," Zircon said.

Rick looked closely at the signature. "If that's Jerry's signature, his writing has really improved since he left school."

Zircon shrugged his shoulders. "He's around somewhere. He couldn't have signed this without showing a pass."

Rick thanked the scientist and rejoined Scotty at the edge of the crowd.

"Why the crinkles in the brow?" Scotty asked as Rick walked toward him.

"I don't know. I guess I'm just jumpy," Rick replied.

"But I'd swear that signature I saw on the reporter list wasn't put there by Jerry Webster."

"Look, pal," Scotty said, putting a hand on Rick's shoulder, "don't start thinking up more trouble just when things are all settled down, will you?"

Rick grinned. "I won't. I wish I could find Jerry though."

They edged their way through the crowd and wandered toward Pirate's Field.

There was a curious group around the launcher. The island scientists were explaining it to those standing near by. As the boys approached, Dr. Wisecarver was saying:

"Prior to this, gentlemen, this experiment would not have been possible because of the lack of a suitable fuel. Had we used gasoline, for instance, more than eight thousand tons would have been needed to throw this rocket into space." He patted the gleaming metal of the base.

The boys joined the crowd, but Rick heard the doctor with only half an ear. He was looking at the faces around him for a sign of Jerry Webster.

"It is necessary," the doctor continued, "for our little baby here to reach a speed of more than seven miles a second in order to break out of the earth's gravitational field."

"But the rocket would burn up at that speed," a voice

objected. "Friction with the atmosphere would heat it to the melting point!"

"That has been taken into consideration," the doctor said. "Since the fuel and the jet engine are controllable by radar, we will start the rocket off at a moderate speed."

A reporter spoke up. "What do you consider a moderate speed, Dr. Wisecarver?"

The doctor's eyes twinkled. "Oh, perhaps two miles a second."

Another reporter had been figuring rapidly on his pad. "Then the rocket will reach the moon in about thirty-five seconds, Doctor?"

"That would be true," Dr. Wisecarver replied, "if we maintained the speed needed to tear it away from the earth's gravity. But you must remember that, large as the moon is, it is a small target when we consider the distance. Therefore we slow the rocket down in order that we may control it better. Hartson Brant has calculated his firing table so that the rocket will take almost a minute and a half to reach the moon."

Rick was familiar with this information and with a jerk of his head he drew Scotty away from the launcher.

"Now what?" Scotty asked.

"Let's take a walk around the island. It'll be some time before the excitement really begins."

Scotty followed him down the path toward the boat

landing. "Maybe we do need a little sea breeze to relax us," he remarked.

As they neared the shore, a strong breeze tugged at their hair and they breathed deeply. "Peace. It's wonderful," Scotty said, smiling.

"Oh, yeah?" Rick was pointing excitedly down toward the dock. "I knew there was something wrong with that signature. Look!"

A few feet off the dock was a figure standing in a rowboat, waving his arms wildly and, obviously, attempting to convince the dock keeper that he belonged on the island. The figure was Jerry Webster!

"Rick!" Jerry shouted as he saw the boys. "Tell this guy who I am!"

Rick ran to the edge of the dock. "It's all right, Mr. Huggins," he said to the island's tenant farmer, who was acting as dock guard. "Come on in, Jerry!"

Jerry pulled on his oars, and as he drew closer, Rick could see an ugly welt across his eye and a bump on his head. His clothing was disheveled as though he had been in a fight.

"What happened?" Rick asked as he reached out to pull the boat into the dock.

"That's what I'd like to know," Jerry panted. "I was supposed to attend this shindig today and I thought I'd get here early. I was walking down the path toward the boat landing on the mainland, when all of a sudden—

boom! I woke up with these." He pointed to his wounds.

Scotty looked at Rick. "You were right," he said. "There's somebody on this island who doesn't belong here."

"If I lay my hands on him—" Jerry stopped and gritted his teeth. "That guy's got my press pass. But the worst of it is, I haven't the faintest idea who he is!"

"I think I have," Rick said. "Only one man in the world would want to get on this island that badly. Scar‑face!"

CHAPTER XXI

Scarface Tries Once More

FOR a moment Scotty and Rick looked at each other.

Then Scotty spoke up. "Scarface must be in the crowd at the laboratory right now."

"Right! And if I know Scarface, he's going to make a last-ditch attempt to wreck the experiment."

They started on a dead run for the laboratory, with Jerry limping along behind. Just as they reached the fringe of the crowd gathered before the rocket launcher, Rick stopped short.

"Oh, what boneheads we are," he said. "Jerry should have stayed out of sight."

"Why?"

"Because if Scarface is in the crowd, he'll see Jerry and know we're wise to him."

"Look, Rick," Scotty said. "This thing is too big for us. Let's tell your father and have the island searched."

Rick peered over the heads of the crowd, trying to locate his father. He spied him, finally, talking to a group of reporters. "Stay here. I'll get him." He edged his way through the crowd toward his father.

As he arrived at the group surrounding his father, he heard him say, "My associates have given me the honor of operating the controls which will launch the rocket. Unfortunately"—he smiled as he spoke—"you cannot stand as near the rocket as you would like to do, for the temperature, at the time the rocket is launched, will be twenty-three hundred degrees Fahrenheit in this spot here."

There were low whistles from the reporters as they scribbled the information on their pads. It was at this moment that Hartson Brant noticed Rick motioning to him from the edge of the crowd.

The scientist excused himself and moved to his son's side.

Rick took the smile from his father's face with two words. "Dad, trouble," he whispered.

Hartson Brant's eyes grew serious. "What is it, Rick?"

Rick took his arm and led him away from the crowd. He told him briefly what had happened to Jerry.

"We must post guards around every installation on the island," Hartson Brant said. "Then we must find the man with Jerry's press pass."

Rick watched his father hurry through the crowd toward the police lieutenant who was assisting in the handling of the crowd. He made his way back to where Scotty and Jerry were standing and told them of his father's decision.

"We're the only ones who have ever seen Scarface," Scotty said. "We'd better help in the search."

Rick nodded. "And you'd better get those bumps fixed up, Jerry," he advised.

"And miss out on a story like this?" Jerry exclaimed. "Not on your life! I'm sticking."

Rick grinned and motioned to the boys to follow. The police were already spreading out through the crowd and a few had stationed themselves about the rocket launcher and the lab. In a moment, the boys were at Hartson Brant's side.

"Let's not be too obvious about this," the scientist was saying to the lieutenant. "I don't want to excite this crowd."

"I get it," the lieutenant said. "Unless he's disguised, it should be easy to find a scar-faced man."

The three boys split up and spread out through the crowd. Rick stared at every face. When he reached the group of men from the Stoneridge Foundation, he peered even more closely. It seemed every one of the dignified gentlemen was wearing a beard. He couldn't go around tugging at all these whiskers to see if they were real, that was certain. But as he wandered innocently through the group of chatting men, he could see that that wouldn't be necessary. There wasn't a false beard in the crowd. Scarface, he decided, would hardly choose so obvious a disguise as a beard, anyway.

Every second the scar-faced man was free, however, meant that much more of a chance for him to do damage. Rick tried hard not to think of what the man might have planned. He quickened his search of the faces and in five minutes had reached the rope stretched before the rocket launcher. It had been installed to keep the crowd back from the delicate mechanism.

He shook his head as he saw Scotty coming toward him. "No sign of him," he said. "How about you?"

"He's not in this crowd," Scotty replied. He looked across Pirate's Field toward the woods. "Do you suppose he'd be hiding in there, waiting his chance?"

"Someone else thought of that," Rick answered, pointing to some plain-clothes men entering the woods. It was more than an hour before the men returned. Rick could see by their faces that the search had been unsuccessful.

Hartson Brant called a conference near the edge of the crowd. "With that man free, we must double our guard," he said. "Heaven knows what he might be planning."

"He won't do much with us around the place," the lieutenant assured him. "Spread out, boys. And keep your eyes open."

The men moved to their stations, and Rick thought

that with the increased guard it would be impossible for Scarface to do anything. But he couldn't convince himself. He had seen too many samples of the scar-faced man's ingenuity in the past. Once more this man was forcing them into a waiting position.

As the afternoon wore on, Rick's tension increased rather than diminished. At least ten times he left the house and wandered through the grounds, hoping to catch a glimpse of the scar-faced man. Each time he returned, Scotty would plead with him to sit down and relax.

The sun was beginning its day's-end plunge in the west and the crowd had begun stirring in anticipation when the three boys left the house together. Since having his wounds dressed, Jerry Webster had been strangely thoughtful. He walked along silently by Rick's side and just as they started to enter the door of the laboratory, he stopped and snapped his fingers loudly.

"I've got it at last!" he exclaimed. "The thing I was trying to think of!"

Rick was jumpy from his tensed nerves and he started slightly. "What are you talking about?" he said.

"Shoes!" Jerry answered. "I saw his shoes as I fell to the ground! They were two-tone browns with funny, hard toes—as if they were reinforced with steel."

"What are we supposed to do, go around looking for shoes instead of faces?" Rick asked.

"Yeah, that'd be silly, wouldn't it," the young reporter answered. "Forget it."

The boys wandered into the lab with a nod to the detective guarding the door. The shadows were growing longer now, and the lab's interior was quite dim. In less than an hour the moon would rise and then the rocket would be launched.

Three workers squatted before the chamber that housed the electron gun. They were dressed in leaded suits and helmets. As the boys came to the door of the room housing the chamber, one of the workers rose and came toward them. It was impossible to tell who it was behind the quartz glass window in the helmet, but when the man raised his hand in salutation, Rick nodded and stood aside to let him pass.

At that moment there was a disturbance at the door behind them. Hobart Zircon was standing in the doorway, waving his arms.

"Clear a path, gentlemen," he announced. "The firing section of the rocket is to be installed now."

The worker who had brushed by them returned to the room and helped the other two men lift a gleaming cylinder from the radiation chamber. Rick knew that the reason for the leaded suits was to protect the workers from the radioactive elements contained in the cylinder. This was the firing section and it emanated invisible deadly rays that would help fire the rocket-fuel mixture.

Hartson Brant moved in beside Hobart Zircon. His eyes moved anxiously over the heavy cylinder and then swung out over the crowd outside the door. Rick knew what was going through his mind. If Scarface were going to make an attempt at sabotage, now would be a good time.

The transfer of the firing section from the lab to the launcher was accomplished without incident, however. The crowd gave the workers a wide berth as they carried it, well knowing that death lay within its walls.

The men reached the edge of the field, where the rocket launcher stood, and set it gingerly in its socket. Then one of the men reached up and unfastened a rope that held the canvas tight around the top part of the rocket.

Silence fell over the crowd as the rocket stood revealed in the last rays of the sun.

Its weight was more than a hundred tons, but the streamlining of the huge space ship made it appear as thin as a pencil. It seemed incredible that enough power could be generated in the tiny firing section to propel this great ship to the moon.

Hartson Brant fidgeted impatiently as the firing section was installed. As soon as danger from radiation was over, he and Hobart Zircon hurried to the foot of the launcher. The crowd pressed close to the ropes, conscious of the drama being unfolded before them. Rick saw his father make a last inspection of the rocket's innards and then nod to Hobart Zircon.

As Hartson Brant turned from the rocket, with a last look at the ship that had taken him so long to bring to reality, Rick knew the emotions that his father must be feeling.

It seemed now that if the scar-faced man had intended to make a last wild attempt to wreck the rocket, his opportunity had passed. The rocket was intact now and the flip of a switch would send it hurtling on its appointed errand, far out into space.

Hartson Brant and Hobart Zircon walked smilingly away from the poised rocket, the three lead-garbed men following. Rick saw one of them stoop, as though making a last inspection of the firing unit, and then his attention was distracted by a commotion at the edge of the crowd.

"What's up?" Scotty exclaimed.

Julius Weiss was pushing through the crowd, followed by a man whom Rick recognized as one of the laboratory workers.

The little scientist was beside himself as he ran to Hartson Brant.

"Hartson!" he cried hoarsely. "Hobart! Listen! I found

Jones in a closet! In a closet, do you hear? There was a noise, and I opened the door, and—"

"Someone slugged me," the workman said. "I was just getting into my suit, and someone sneaked up behind me. I woke up in the closet, tied up."

"Scarface!"

Everyone looked at Rick as he uttered the name, comprehension dawning in their faces. Scarface had knocked Jones unconscious and then taken his suit!

"The shoes," Jerry Webster yelled suddenly. "The shoes! Look!" He was pointing at the feet of one of the lead-helmeted workers, who was just walking away from the crowd.

Rick stared at the feet of the worker.

The man's shoes were two-toned brown and equipped with hard toes!

"It's him!" Jerry Webster yelled. "It's the guy that slugged me!"

The man in the leaded suit suddenly broke into a run. He reached for the bulky helmet, attempting to wrench it off. With a vault, Scotty was over the ropes and sprinting after the running figure. A flying tackle brought the man down with a crash.

Into the dirt they went, the hooded man struggling with his helmet. The force of Scotty's tackle wrenched off the two heavy clasps and the helmet came free. In desperation, the man swung it high over his head and aimed it squarely at Scotty's face.

The vicious blow was never completed, for as the man's arm drew back, Scotty's fist shot forward, straight into the pit of his stomach. Heavy as the cloth of the suit was, it could not protect the man from the paralyzing force of the punch. With a painful whoosh of escaping breath, his arm flopped to his side and the helmet rolled away.

A second punch landed and his whole body went limp. Hartson Brant, Rick, and Jerry Webster were the first ones to reach Scotty's side. He was sitting astride the figure in the leaded suit, pointing a finger straight at the man's face.

"Scarface," he said simply.

Hartson Brant looked into the scarred face and let out a shocked gasp.

"Manfred Wessel!"

A long-forgotten memory flashed into Rick's mind. No wonder he had thought this scarred face familiar. Manfred Wessel had once worked for his father, many years before. Then he had drifted away and had been heard of next in Germany. He was suspected of aiding in the development of the Nazi rocket bombs, but since precise proof was lacking, he had not been indicted as a war criminal. Later he had turned up in America and had applied to Hartson Brant for a position on the island staff. Naturally, he had been refused.

Somehow, since then, he had been badly scarred. Rick guessed that a chemical explosion had been responsible. No wonder Wessel had been familiar yet unrecognizable.

"You were the one," Hartson Brant accused. "You were duplicating our experiment, and when the time came, you were going to step forth and claim credit, after first destroying our rocket. Until now, Manfred Wessel, the world of science has had only strong suspicions of your dealings, but this, I think, will be ample proof."

He must have sneaked into the lab as soon as he got on the island, Rick thought, and waited for an opportunity. Scarface would have known that some of the workers would be dressed in the shield suits, and he had hidden himself, perhaps in the very closet where he had put Jones.

Wessel stood with slumped shoulders, the picture of despair.

"The rest of your gang is already behind bars," Hartson Brant continued. "I think our police lieutenant will gladly take you to join them."

Suddenly Wessel made a driving leap. He broke through the surprised ring of spectators and ran through the orchard toward the air strip.

Instantly Rick and Scotty were after him, outdistancing the older men. But Wessel's move had taken them by surprise and he had a good lead.

"The plane," Scotty gasped. "He'll try to get away in the Cub!"

"No," Rick said breathlessly. "He couldn't start it in time."

Wessel swerved and ran in an arc that would take him to the south shore, behind the laboratory. The boys were gaining now, running for all they were worth. Behind them they heard the cries of the others.

They passed the lab and Rick yelled, "Go right, Scotty!" He himself turned left, realizing that Wessel was approaching the south cliff. They would cut him off.

But the renegade was running toward the sea, not trying to reach safety. Rick put on a burst of speed and saw that Scotty was gaining, too.

Manfred Wessel reached the cliff and leaped far out into space!

The boys stopped short at the bluff and looked down at the creaming surf that shattered against the island. They turned away, feeling sick. Nothing could live in that rock-fanged sea!

Hartson Brant came up with the others and looked silently down at the surf.

"He was a disgrace to the sciences," Mr. Brant said, as

he turned away, "and he was a dangerous man. But I would not wish to see him end that way."

On the heels of his statement Rick exclaimed, "Dad, the launcher! I saw him hanging back when the rest of you left."

He and Scotty led the rush back to the field where the gleaming moon rocket rested in its high cradle. There, at the base, Hartson Brant found a small box. He ripped the cover off and touched the mass of gelatin within. Then, with an angry gesture, he ripped loose the wires that connected the box to the cylinder.

"Phrenodyne," he said in a hushed voice. "The fastest-acting explosive known."

"His plan is clear," Zircon boomed. "The phrenodyne would have acted a split second before the rocket fuel exploded—just soon enough to shatter the base and send the rocket off at an angle too acute to be corrected by our instruments. We would surely have missed the target."

"And lost the grant," Hartson Brant added. "Then Wessel would have made a try."

"But the plan didn't succeed," little Julius Weiss put in. "Thanks to our young friends here."

A shaggy little figure trotted up, late as usual. "Don't forget Dismal," Rick smiled.

Then they were all walking back toward the lab, except for the reporters who were running for telephones to report the sensational development.

"I wonder if Wessel knew—" Scotty mused.

"Knew what?"

"Nothing. Only he didn't seem like the kind of man who would commit suicide."

"He did, though," Rick answered. He shuddered. "We saw him. Let's not talk about it any more, huh? Let's go shoot our rocket."

"Okay," Scotty said. "Only— Well, never mind."

CHAPTER XXII

The Launching of the Rocket

THERE was a hushed silence in the main room of the big laboratory. Rick found himself holding his breath as Barby leaned over the control panel where his father was seated.

"This one, Daddy?" she asked.

"That one, Barby," Hartson Brant said.

Barby threw the switch.

For a tense instant there was silence; then a mighty, diminishing roar shook the island. It was echoed by a great shout from the assembled watchers.

The moon rocket was on its way!

Rick, with Scotty and Jerry close on his heels, ran for the stairs. He paused long enough to pat Barby on the shoulder and exclaim, "Good shooting, Sis."

At Rick's suggestion, the honor of firing the rocket had been given to Barby, although Hartson Brant had first offered it to the two boys.

He went up the flight of stairs and burst out on the roof where the observatory was set up. Julius Weiss hunched over the eyepiece of a large telescope and there was exultation in the very set of his small body.

Without taking his eye away, he said, "I have it. I see the trail perfectly."

Rick's glance sought the moon, which was rising above the horizon. Out there was the rocket, speeding through infinite space.

"Professor Weiss," he asked, "may we have a look?"

Julius Weiss tore himself away from the precious sight. "I mustn't be selfish. But quickly, boys, quickly!"

One after another, Rick, Scotty, and Jerry saw the fiery trail that was a faint line against the dark of the heavens. Then they relinquished the telescope to Weiss and ran back downstairs.

Hartson Brant bent over his controls, his eyes riveted to the instruments and to his radar screen.

Hobart Zircon sat before a larger screen, a big oval that glowed with a greenish light. On it were two bands of light from which little pulsations flickered.

Without looking up, he indicated the largest point of light. "This 'blip' is the moon." His index finger chose a second, smaller point. "The rocket."

The boys stood very still, watching. The smaller "blip" was moving with deceptive slowness across the screen to the larger one.

They were getting closer. Now there were only inches between them. Now only fractions . . .

They merged!

From the roof came a piercing shout. The boys charged back up the stairs to find Julius Weiss doing a very unscientific war dance.

"A direct hit," he shouted joyously. "Oh, beautiful! Beautiful! Right in the Mare Imbrium. I saw the explosion. I saw it! Oh, magnificent!"

"What's the Mare Imbrium?" Jerry Webster asked dazedly.

No one bothered to explain that it was the largest flat plain on the moon. They were all running downstairs again to where men crowded around a flushed and happy Hartson Brant.

"Hartson," a distinguished-looking man was saying, "there can be no doubt that the grant goes to you and your associates."

"Did you hear that, Scotty?"

"I heard it, Rick. It's great!"

"You have proved that radar control of a projectile is possible at great distances beyond the atmosphere. This may very well be the pioneer step that will someday see the first man on the moon's surface."

"I want to take a look," Rick whispered. "Come on."

With Scotty, he hurried back to the telescope on the roof. Rick looked first, long and searchingly.

"Right in the center," he said. "Take a look, Scotty."

Scotty applied his eye to the opening. "Where? Oh, that dark spot? It looks like a shadow."

"That's it." Rick was exultant. "The new crater caused by the explosion. That's the rocket's shadow, old son!"

As they solemnly shook hands, a burly figure joined them.

It was Hobart Zircon. "Well, lads," he said, "I think we can start packing our bags, now that this is over."

Rick saw the twinkle in the huge scientist's eyes. "Start packing, sir?"

"Yes, for a short trip." Zircon smiled. He pointed to the moon, which rode so serenely above the horizon. "We're not through with old Luna yet. It might be exciting. Although I suppose both of you have had enough excitement for the present?"

"No, sir," they said.

Hobart Zircon beckoned them closer and lowered his voice. "Our next stop is high Tibet, half the world away. Lads, we're going to set up a moon relay!"

RICK BRANT and his friend Scotty accompany a scientific expedition to Tibet in the next volume, THE LOST CITY. Don't miss this thrilling story of mystery and adventure in a strange, forbidden city lost in the Himalayas.

F
B   25,587

AUTHOR
Blaine, John

TITLE
The rocket's shadow.

F
B   25,587

Blaine ,John

The rocket's shadow.